Skellig

THE PLAY

ALSO BY DAVID ALMOND

Skellig

Kit's Wilderness

Heaven Eyes

Counting Stars

Secret Heart

The Fire-Eaters

Wild Girl, Wild Boy (play)

DAVID ALMOND

Skellig

THE PLAY

Delacorte Press

Published by Delacorte Press, an imprint of Random House Children's Books, a division of Random House, Inc., New York

Visit us on the Web! www.randomhouse.com/kids
Educators and librarians, for a variety of teaching tools, visit us at
www.randomhouse.com/teachers

Library of Congress Cataloging-in-Publication Data

Almond, David.
[Skellig]
Two plays / David Almond.
p. cm.
Contents: Skellig—Wild girl, wild boy.
ISBN 0-385-73074-8—ISBN 0-385-90101-1
1. Children's plays, English. I. Almond, David, Wild girl, wild boy. II. Title.
PR6051.L588S57 2005
822'.914—dc22 2004061750

The text of this book is set in 12-point Minion.

Book design by Angela Carlino

Printed in the United States of America

November 2005

10 9 8 7 6 5 4 3 2 1

BVG

INTRODUCTION

One of the joys of writing for young people is that they don't recognize the supposed boundaries between different forms of storytelling. Tell a child the story of Hansel and Gretel and pretty soon, given the opportunity, the child will tiptoe through the house as if the house were a forest, will peer through doorways as if towards a gingerbread house, will open a cupboard as if the cupboard were a lethal oven. And will whisper and scream and groan and tremble with fear and yell with delight. And will drag in other characters: "Be the wicked witch, Mummy! Sneak away and leave me in the forest, Dad." Tell the story of Cinderella, and the ballroom will be made to appear in the twenty-first-century living room. The story of Red Riding Hood will set the wolf prowling and howling in even the most neatly tended garden. So fiction will flow fluidly into drama, into dance, into song.

Books, with their neat lines of print and their beautifully bound pages, appear to be orderly, modern, civilized, but we shouldn't forget that their roots are ancient. Stories on the page are indissolubly linked to the stories chanted in firelit caves at the beginning of human time. They grow out of myth and ritual and sorcery and spell. They predate the print and the pages in which they appear to be caught. Stories (like children?)

are only semicivilized. They retain a wildness at their heart.

The story of *Skellig* came out of the blue. I was walking through a town called Reigate one sunny afternoon when it all started to tell itself in my head. "I found him in the garage on a Sunday afternoon." When I started to write it down, when Michael stepped for the first time into the dangerous garage, it often seemed that the story was writing itself. I was never quite sure where it had come from, where it was going, where it would end. It kept growing, evolving, like a living thing. I sometimes wonder, What if I'd walked down a different street in a different town? What if it had been another day? What if it had been cloudy? What would the story have been then? Would there have been a story at all? No answers, of course. The ways of the imagination are mysterious. Six months after I'd started it, it was complete. A year or so after that, there it was, beautiful printed pages caught between covers. A finished thing, or so I thought. Just after it was published, I read a few pages to a roomful of children in a local school. At the end of the session, two boys rushed up to me. "We're going to act out *Skellig* in the yard. Daniel's Michael. I'm Skellig. Lucy! Come and be Mina!" And they ran off to act the story out, and in doing so, they taught me something (as children often do) about how stories work. For them, the story on the page was just the start.

When the children ran out into the yard, they were running out in order to play—with their bodies, their minds, their imaginations. It's no coincidence that plays are called plays, that actors are referred to as players. All art is a form of play, a passionate blend of seriousness and fun. The writer at his desk is like a scribbling child. Actors in rehearsal are like children at play in the schoolyard. Not long after the two boys in the classroom proposed making a play out of my story, I was contacted by Trevor Nunn with a very similar proposal, but this time the play would be performed on a stage rather than in a schoolyard. It was the beginning of a long and complicated journey. A couple of times the project seemed doomed to fail. Was it possible to make this work onstage? Was it even desirable? I was asked several times: Aren't you afraid that the story will be diminished? Are you not scared that it'll be spoiled? These questions never worried me. Right from our first discussions, through the first exploratory workshops, through all the project's stops and starts, I saw how the story that had first come to life in Reigate continued to grow and evolve and to assume a new and fascinating shape. The words were simply a seed. Trevor Nunn and his astounding team of actors, designers and composers nurtured the tale and brought it into a new and vivid incarnation. I saw that the story, in being lifted so beautifully away from the page, was allowed to draw fully on its magical ritualistic roots. And when the play opened, and Michael stepped into the garage in the dark space of the Young Vic, we were all returned to the firelit caves again, and all around, the watching faces glowed.

Skellig—The Play

was first performed on 21st November 2003

at the Young Vic, 66 The Cut, London SE1.

DIRECTION—Trevor Nunn

DESIGN—John Napier

LIGHTING—Howard Harrison

MUSIC—Shaun Davey

SOUND—Fergus O'Hare

COSTUMES—Elise Napier

MOVEMENT—Kate Flatt

Cast in alphabetical order:

COOT—Ashley Artus

MUM—Cathryn Bradshaw

DAD—Antony Byrne

MISS CLARTS/LUCY CARR—Sarah Cattle

MRS. MCKEE—Noma Dumezweni

MINA—Akiya Henry

DR. MCNABOLA/RASPUTIN—William Osborne

SKELLIG—David Threlfall

MICHAEL—Kevin Wathen

LEAKY—Mo Zainal

UNDERSTUDIES—Chris Lennon & Cherry Menlove

Characters
(in order of appearance)

Mr. Stone

Dad

Mum

Michael

Skellig

Rasputin

The Yeti

Miss Clarts

Leakey

Coot

Mina

Lucy Carr

Nurse

Old Woman

Dr. McNabola

Mrs. McKee

ACT ONE

NARRATION Just imagine,

NARRATION Said Mr. Stone.

MR. STONE You have to see it with your mind's eye.

NARRATION They called it a garage because that was what Mr. Stone, the estate agent, called it.

MR. STONE See it cleaned, with new doors and the roof repaired. See it as a wonderful two-car garage. Or something for you, lad—a hideaway for you and your mates. . . .

MICHAEL It was more like a demolition site.

MR. STONE Just see it with your mind's eye. Just imagine what could be done.

NARRATION All the way round the house, Michael kept thinking of the old man, Ernie Myers, who had lived there on his own for years.

MR. STONE He'd been dead nearly a week before they found him under a table in the kitchen.

MICHAEL That was what I saw when Stone told us about seeing with the mind's eye.

NARRATION	He even said it when they got to the dining room.
NARRATION	There was an old cracked toilet sitting there in the corner, behind a plywood screen.
MR. STONE	Towards the end, Ernie couldn't manage the stairs, so his bed was brought in here, and a toilet, so everything was easy for him.
MICHAEL	I wanted to get back to our old house again and back to my mates Leaky and Coot and a football match that lasted all day.
LEAKY & COOT	On me head! On me head!
MICHAEL	But Mum and Dad just took it all in. They went on like it was some big game.
DAD	I'll get that cornice back there. And dado. Aye, dado, that's the stuff. This wall, now. Imagine it gone, love. Whack! Imagine the space we'd open up.
MUM	And there's a perfect little nursery.
DAD	I'll paint a goal for him on the outside wall. I'll put a swing up for

	the little'n. And a blinking pond, eh? Fish and frogs and . . .
MUM	Not too soon, though. Don't want any dangers in her way.
DAD	No, that's right, no dangers. Like that garage, eh? That'll have to come down. Whack! A lovely bit of knocky down.
MUM	Could we get it done in time?
DAD	The basics, definitely. It's just routine, love. I can see it all. We'll get it ready. We'll get moved in. Then the baby'll come. Perfect, eh?
MUM	We'd be moving just in time for spring. . . .
DAD	It'll be a big adventure.
NARRATION	They bought the house.
NARRATION	They started cleaning it
NARRATION	And scrubbing it
NARRATION	And painting it,
NARRATION	Getting ready to move in.

MUM	Ouch!
DAD	What's up, love? Love, what's up?
MUM	Oh!
NARRATION	Then the baby came too early.
NARRATION	And she was already with them when they moved.
NARRATION	And there they were.
MICHAEL	And here we are.

NARRATION	So, it was the day after they moved in to Falconer Road.
NARRATION	It was still winter.
NARRATION	The others were inside the house with Doctor Dan, worrying about the baby.
MICHAEL	I called him Doctor Death.
NARRATION	Nobody else was there.
MICHAEL	Just me.

MICHAEL moves towards the garage

NARRATION The timbers were rotten and the roof was sagging in.

NARRATION It stank of rot and dust.

NARRATION It was like the whole place was sick of itself.

MICHAEL is about to slip inside.

MUM Michael! What you doing? Didn't we tell you to keep out? Well, didn't we?

MICHAEL Yes.

MUM So keep out! All right? All right?

MICHAEL All right. Yes. All right. All right.

MUM Do you not think we've got more to worry about than stupid you getting crushed in a stupid garage?

MICHAEL Yes.

MUM You just keep out then. Right?

MICHAEL Right, Right, right, right, right. Then I went back to the wilderness we called a garden and Mum went back to the flaming baby.

MUM — *(off)* Michael, are you coming in for lunch?

MICHAEL — No, I'm staying in the garden. The garden! There was going to be benches and a table and a swing and a goalpost painted on the wall of the house. But there was none of that. I stood there, kicking the heads off a million dandelions.

Mum brings Michael a can of Coke.

MUM — Oh, Michael. Sorry it's all so rotten and we're all in such rotten moods. You understand, though, don't you? Don't you?

MICHAEL — Yes.

Mum goes back inside.

MICHAEL — I finished the Coke, waited a minute, then went back to the garage. I didn't have time to dare myself or to stand there listening to the scratching. I switched the torch on, took a deep breath and tiptoed inside.

NARRATION — Something little and black scuttled across the floor.

NARRATION	The door creaked and cracked for a moment before it was still.
NARRATION	Dust poured through the torch beam.
NARRATION	He felt spiderwebs breaking on his brow.
NARRATION	Everything was packed in tight.
NARRATION	Ancient furniture.
NARRATION	Kitchen units,
NARRATION	Rolled-up carpets.
NARRATION	Pipes
NARRATION	And crates
NARRATION	And planks.
NARRATION	He kept ducking down under the hose pipes and ropes and kit bags that hung from the roof.
NARRATION	The floor was broken and crumbly.
NARRATION	He opened a cupboard an inch, shone the torch in and . . .
NARRATION	Saw a million woodlice scattering away.

NARRATION	He peered down into a great stone jar and saw
MICHAEL	The bones of some little animal that had died in there.
NARRATION	Dead bluebottles were everywhere.
NARRATION	There were ancient newspapers and magazines.
NARRATION	He shone the torch on one and saw that it came from nearly
MICHAEL	Fifty years ago.
NARRATION	He was scared every moment that the whole thing was going to collapse.
NARRATION	There was dust clogging his throat and nose.
NARRATION	He knew they'd be yelling for him soon,
NARRATION	And he knew he'd better get out.
NARRATION	He leaned across a heap of tea chests
NARRATION	And shone the torch into the space behind and . . .

Michael shines the torch onto Skellig.

SKELLIG What do you want?

What do you want?

I said, What do you want?

DAD Michael! Michael!

Michael backs out.

DAD Michael, man!

MICHAEL I know. I know.

DAD It's for your own damn good.

Dad thumps the side of the trembling garage.

DAD Imagine what might happen.

Dad thumps the side of the garage again.

DAD Imagine.

Michael grabs his arm, stops him.

MICHAEL Don't. I understand.

DAD It's coming down, the first damn chance I get.

MICHAEL	Is she going to die, Dad?
DAD	Die? What do you mean, die? Dan's just told us—she's doing fine. They'd have her in hospital if she wasn't. Wouldn't they? Well, wouldn't they? Come on, get that dust off before your mother sees.

In the kitchen.

NARRATION	The next morning before breakfast.
MICHAEL	What's going to happen to the garage now? When are they going to clear it out?
DAD	When we can get someone to come. It's not important, son, not now.
MICHAEL	OK. Shall I stay off school so I can help?
DAD	Aye, you can take Ernie's toilet out and scrub the floorboards round it.
MICHAEL	I'll go to school.

MICHAEL	I wanted to stay at Kenny Street High, with Leaky and Coot, so I didn't mind that I had to get the bus through town. I watched the people getting on and off,
NARRATION	Reading their papers,
NARRATION	Picking their nails,
NARRATION	Looking dreamily out the windows.
MICHAEL	You could never know, by looking at them, what was happening in their lives.
NARRATION	He wanted to stand up and say,
MICHAEL	My sister is ill and it's the first day I've traveled on the bus from the new house to the old school, and . . . and . . . there's a man in our garage!
NARRATION	But he didn't.
NARRATION	He just went on looking at all the faces and swinging back and forward when the bus swung round corners.
MICHAEL	I knew if someone looked at me, they'd know nothing about me either.

Bus bell.

School bell rings.

In school assembly:

RASPUTIN Come along now. Lift up your hearts and voices.

(Sings) All things bright and beautiful,

All creatures great and small . . .

School bell rings.

In the school corridors:

THE YETI Keep to the left, you horrible people! Leakey and Coot! Keep your feet to yourselves, you horrible pair!

School bell rings.

In the classroom:

MISS CLARTS And, oh, it was so sad. Poor poor Icarus. He was young and bold and without fear. He flew so high, almost to the sun, and the wax melted and his feathers fell away from his arms, and he began to tumble through the air. He dropped like a stone past his father, Daedalus, into the deep blue sea. . . . Now, there's a story for you, Michael. . . . Michael?

NARRATION But Michael couldn't concentrate.

NARRATION Not with so much going on.

School bell rings.

NARRATION He couldn't even concentrate on football.

A football game.

LEAKEY On me head! On me head! Yeah! It's in!

COOT It's not! It didn't cross the line!

LEAKEY It did, man, it did! It was miles over! Wasn't it, Michael? Michael?

NARRATION He walked to the edge of the field and stared over the town towards his new home.

LEAKEY What's up with him?

COOT Who knows? He was always a bit . . .

MISS CLARTS You OK, Michael?

MICHAEL Fine, Miss.

MISS CLARTS And the baby?

MICHAEL Fine too.

MISS CLARTS If there's anything you need to talk about . . .

MICHAEL No. No, Miss. Nothing.

Michael runs and slide tackles Coot.

MICHAEL It did cross the line! It did cross the bloody line!

School bell rings.

Home, same afternoon.

DAD Michael! Come here. Look. Hold your nose.

He sits on the toilet and grins.

DAD Make a nice water feature, eh? Or a garden ornament.

Hey, and have a look at this. Ready?

He picks up a carrier bag of dead pigeons, shows them to MICHAEL.

MICHAEL Yuk. What are they?

DAD Dead pigeons. Found them behind that old gas fire. Look at this one.

MICHAEL That's a pigeon?

DAD Aye. Been there a long time, that's all. Nearly a fossil. Feel it. Go on, it's OK.

MICHAEL It's hard as stone.

DAD That's right. Hard as stone and black as blinking coal. School was OK?

MICHAEL Aye. Leakey and Coot said they might come over on Sunday.

DAD Great! Just what you need.

MICHAEL *continues to inspect the pigeon in his hands. He throws it up, catches it, feels its dead weight, throws it up again.*

MICHAEL	Where's the baby?
DAD	Eh?
MICHAEL	Where's Mam? Where's the baby?
DAD	At the hospital.
MICHAEL	The hospital?
DAD	Just a checkup, man. Look, I'm going to have a bath. I'll make tea for when they're back. It's routine, son. Little baby, few days old . . .
	(sings) Take me back to the Black Hills,
	The Black Hills of Dakota.
MICHAEL	My hands were trembling.
NARRATION	He went out past Ernie's toilet,
NARRATION	The old gas fire,
NARRATION	The dead pigeons.
NARRATION	And tiptoed inside.
NARRATION	He told himself,

MICHAEL I'm stupid.

NARRATION He told himself,

MICHAEL I'm dreaming.

NARRATION He told himself,

MICHAEL I won't see him again.

NARRATION But he did.

MICHAEL shines the torch on SKELLIG's face.

SKELLIG You again?

MICHAEL What you doing there?

SKELLIG Nothing. Nothing, nothing and nothing.

MICHAEL They're coming to clear the rubbish out. They're going to knock the whole place down.

SKELLIG You got an aspirin?

MICHAEL An aspirin?

SKELLIG Never mind.

MICHAEL You're not Ernie Myers, are you?

SKELLIG That old git? Coughing his guts and spewing everywhere.

MICHAEL Sorry.

SKELLIG What do you want?

MICHAEL Nothing.

SKELLIG You got an aspirin?

MICHAEL No.

SKELLIG Thanks very much.

MICHAEL What will you do? It'll all cave in on you.

SKELLIG Nothing. Go away.

MICHAEL You could come inside.

SKELLIG laughs but doesn't smile.

SKELLIG Go away.

SKELLIG picks a bluebottle from the front of his suit and pops it in his mouth.

MICHAEL Is there something I could bring you?

SKELLIG An aspirin.

MICHAEL Something you'd like to eat?

SKELLIG 27 and 53.

MICHAEL What?

SKELLIG Nothing. Go away. Go away.

MICHAEL backs away, out of the garage, and hears his dad singing "The Black Hills of Dakota" in the bath. A blackbird sings. MINA's head appears over the top of the wall into the back lane.

MINA Are you the new boy here?

MICHAEL spins.

MINA Are you the new boy here?

MICHAEL Yes.

MINA I'm Mina. Well?

MICHAEL Well, what?

MINA clicks her tongue and shakes her head.

MINA I'm Mina, you're . . .

MICHAEL Michael.

MINA Good. *(She jumps down.)* Nice to meet you, Michael.

MINA disappears behind the garden wall.

DAD *(Sings) . . . the beautiful Indian country that I love.*

NARRATION When he came down from his bath, Dad started moaning.

DAD There's no bread, no eggs, not a bit of decent nosh.

NARRATION And in the end he said . . .

DAD I know, let's have a takeaway.

NARRATION He took the menu for the Chinese round the corner out of the drawer.

DAD We'll get it in for when your mum gets back. What d'you fancy?

MICHAEL 27 and 53!

DAD That's clever. You did that without looking. What's your next trick? *(He writes.)* Special chow mein for Mum, spring rolls and pork char sui for you, beef and mushroom for me, crispy seaweed and prawn crackers for the baby. And if she won't eat them, we will, and serve her right, eh? She'll be back on boring mother's milk again.

MICHAEL I ran round to collect it.

At the Chinese takeaway:

NARRATION Spring roll, pork char sui, prawn cracker, special chow mein, beef and mushroom. OK.

MICHAEL returns with the food. MUM and the baby are home again.

MUM Hello! We're home again!

They eat at the table.

MUM School was OK, then?

MICHAEL Aye, fine.

MUM And the journey?

MICHAEL Fine and all.

MUM Good lad.

MICHAEL Is she OK?

MUM Aye. They're keeping an eye on her, though.

DAD eats voraciously, swigs brown ale.

DAD — Champion nosh, eh?

He sees MICHAEL has left some food on his plate, reaches for it.

DAD — Aha! Extra 27 and 53!

MICHAEL covers his food with his arm.

MICHAEL — You'll get fat.

MUM — Fatt*er*!

DAD — I'm famished. Worked like a slave for you lot today.

He reaches out and tickles the baby.

DAD — Specially for you, little chick.

MICHAEL — Fatso.

DAD grabs his belly.

MUM — See?

DAD dips his finger into the sauce at the edge of MICHAEL's plate, licks his finger.

DAD — Delicious. But enough's enough. I've had an ample sufficiency, thank you.

DAD goes to the fridge, takes out brown ale.

DAD Now, where's that cheese?

MICHAEL clears the dishes, puts what is left of 27 and 53 into the waste bin.

NARRATION He put what was left of 27 and 53 in the outside bin.

NARRATION And he saw Mina again,

NARRATION Sitting in a tree.

MICHAEL I'm just going out for a while!

No answer. MUM and DAD are engrossed in the baby.

MICHAEL goes to MINA. He stands beneath her in her garden.

MICHAEL What you doing up there?

MINA Silly you. You've scared it away. Typical!

MICHAEL Scared what away?

MINA The blackbird.

She drops to the ground.

MINA Never mind. It'll come again.

The blackbird squawks.

MINA That's its warning call. It's telling its family there's danger near. Danger. That's you. There's three tiny ones in a nest up there. But don't you dare go any nearer. This is where I live. Number 7. You've got a baby sister.

MICHAEL Yes.

MINA What's her name?

MICHAEL We haven't decided yet.

MINA clicks her tongue. She opens her sketchbook and shows MICHAEL what's inside.

MINA This is the blackbird. Common, but nevertheless very beautiful. A sparrow. These are tits. And look, this is the goldfinch that visited last Thursday.

MINA slaps the book shut.

MINA Do you like birds?

MICHAEL I don't know.

MINA Typical. Do you like drawing?

MICHAEL Sometimes.

MINA Drawing helps you to see the world more clearly. Did you know that? What color's a blackbird?

MICHAEL Black.

MINA Typical. I'm going inside. I look forward to seeing you again. I'd also like to see your baby sister if that can be arranged.

MICHAEL I tried to stay awake that night.

NARRATION But it was hopeless.

NARRATION He was dreaming straightaway.

NARRATION He was dreaming that the baby was in the blackbird's nest in Mina's garden.

NARRATION The blackbird fed her on flies . . .

NARRATION And spiders . . .

NARRATION — And she got stronger until she flew out of the tree . . .

NARRATION — And over the rooftops and onto the garage roof.

NARRATION — Mina sat on the back wall drawing her.

NARRATION — When he got closer, Mina whispered,

MINA — Stay away! You're danger!

Baby crying and MUM *cooing.*

NARRATION — Then the baby started bawling in the room next door,

MICHAEL — And I woke up.

DAD *snoring, baby crying,* MUM *cooing, birdsong.*

MICHAEL — Aspirin.

MICHAEL *gets out of bed, fetches the aspirin from the table drawer and goes outside. He retrieves the takeaway from the waste bin and goes towards the garage. He switches on his torch.*

MICHAEL — I must be stupid. I must be going round the stupid bend.

He creeps into the garage, comes to SKELLIG.

SKELLIG You again? Thought you'd gone away.

MICHAEL I've brought something. Aspirin. And number 27 and 53. Spring rolls and pork char sui.

SKELLIG Not as stupid as you look.

He reaches for the trays but he is too weak.

SKELLIG No strength.

MICHAEL *holds the trays while* SKELLIG *eats.*

SKELLIG Aaaah. Ooooooh. Put the aspirin in.

MICHAEL *puts them in the Chinese sauce and* SKELLIG *swallows them. He belches and slumps back against the wall.*

SKELLIG Food of the gods. 27 and 53.

MICHAEL *stares at him.*

SKELLIG Had a good look?

MICHAEL Where you from?

SKELLIG Nowhere.

MICHAEL It's coming down. What will you do?

SKELLIG Nothing, nothing and nothing. Leave the aspirin.

MICHAEL puts the jar on the floor and has to push aside a little heap of hard furry balls. MICHAEL holds one up to the torchlight.

SKELLIG What you looking at, eh?

MICHAEL Nothing. There's a doctor comes to see my sister. I could bring him here to see you.

SKELLIG No doctors. Nobody.

MICHAEL Who are you?

SKELLIG Nobody.

MICHAEL What can I do?

SKELLIG Nothing.

MICHAEL My baby sister's really ill.

SKELLIG Babies!

MICHAEL Is there anything you can do for her?

SKELLIG Babies! Spittle, muck, spew and tears.

MICHAEL	My name's Michael. I'm going now. Is there anything else I can bring you?
SKELLIG	Nothing. 27 and 53.

Skellig retches. Michael puts his hand beneath his shoulder to steady him.

MICHAEL	Who are you? I wouldn't tell anybody.
SKELLIG	I'm nearly nobody. Most of me is Arthur. Arthur Itis. He's the one that's ruining me bones. Turns you to stone, then crumbles you away.
MICHAEL	What's on your back?
SKELLIG	A jacket, then a bit of me, then lots and lots of Arthur.

Michael tries to slip his hand under Skellig's jacket.

SKELLIG	No good. Nothing there's no good no more.
MICHAEL	I'll go. I'll keep them from clearing the place out. I'll bring you more. I won't bring Doctor Death.
SKELLIG	27 and 53. 27 and 53.

MICHAEL leaves the garage.

MICHAEL — I felt something beneath his shoulder. Like . . . like . . .

NARRATION — And then he tiptoed back to bed.

The next morning.

DAD — Where's those aspirin?

MUM — All this exercise'll do him good. It'll get that fat off him.

DAD — I said where's those blooming aspirin? I can hardly move, my back's killing me, I'm stiff as a blinking board.

MUM — You need some cod-liver oil!

She looks in the table drawer, takes out some capsules.

MUM — Here you are. Get a couple of these down you.

DAD — Yuk!

At school. Michael, Leaky, Coot and others in the classroom.

NARRATION That morning they had science with Rasputin.

NARRATION He showed them a poster of our ancestors,

NARRATION Of the endless shape-changing that has led to us.

RASPUTIN We start off in the primeval soup. We're little cell-like things, then fishy things, froggy things, then things that crawl out onto land. We start to look a bit like us. Ape-like things, monkey-like things. There's the main route, but there's also false tracks, wrong turnings, routes that led to nothing. Hominid. *Australopithecus.* Neanderthal. *Homo erectus.* See how we stand straighter, how we lose our hair, how we start to use tools, how our heads change shape to hold our great brains . . . like yours, Mr. Coot.

MICHAEL Sir!

RASPUTIN Michael?

MICHAEL Will we always keep on changing?

RASPUTIN	Who knows, Michael? Maybe we're in the process of evolving right now, but we don't know it yet. . . .
COOT	Bollocks!
RASPUTIN	Now, I want you to draw the skeleton of an ape and the skeleton of a man.
MICHAEL	Sir!
RASPUTIN	Michael?
MICHAEL	What are shoulder blades for, sir?
RASPUTIN	I know what my mother used to tell me, but to be honest, I haven't a clue.

School bell rings. End of lesson.

COOT	What a load of rubbish.
LEAKEY	Eh?
COOT	It's bollocks, man. My dad says there's no way that monkeys can turn into men. Just got to look at them. Stands to reason, man.

Coot hunches his shoulders up and runs at the girls.

LUCY CARR Stop it, you pig!

COOT Pig? I'm not a pig. I'm a gorilla!

MICHAEL, LEAKEY and COOT play football.

LEAKY On me head! On me head! Michael, man! What's wrong? You're playing crap.

School bell.

On the bus, going home.

NARRATION Time for the bus.

NARRATION Back and forward.

NARRATION Home to school. School to home.

NARRATION He took his skeleton picture home.

NARRATION He kept looking at it on the bus.

NARRATOR An old bloke was sitting beside him with a Jack Russell on his knee.

NARRATOR He smelt of pee and pipe smoke.

OLD MAN	What's that?
MICHAEL	Picture of what we used to be like long ago.
OLD MAN	Can't say I remember that, and I'm pretty ancient. I saw a monkey in a circus in my young days. They'd trained it to make tea but it was nothing like a person, really. But maybe it was just practicing.
MICHAEL	There's . . . there's a man in our garage.
OLD MAN	Aye? And there was the loveliest lass on the trapeze. You could swear she could nearly fly.

Bus stops. MICHAEL runs home.

NARRATOR	Back at home, there was bad news.
MUM	It's this damn place! How can she thrive when it's all in such a mess? See what I mean? Bloody stupid toilet! Bloody ruins! A bloody stupid wilderness. We should never have come to this stinking derelict place. My little girl. My poor little girl.

DAD — The baby has to go to hospital.

MICHAEL — The hospital?

DAD — Just for a while. She'll be fine. It's routine. I'll work harder. I'll get it all ready for when she comes home again.

MICHAEL — I'll help.

DAD — That's good.

Mum packs baby clothes into a suitcase. Michael watches.

MUM — Try not to worry, love. It won't be for long.

MICHAEL — Mum.

MUM — Yes?

MICHAEL — What are shoulder blades for?

MUM — Oh, Michael!

Mum pushes past Michael, then stops. She slips her fingers under his shoulder blades.

MUM — They say that shoulder blades are where your wings were, when you were an angel. They say they're

	where your wings will grow again one day.
MICHAEL	It's just a story, though. A fairy tale for little kids. Isn't it?
MUM	Who knows? Maybe one day we all had wings and one day we'll all have wings again.
MICHAEL	D'you think the baby had wings?
MUM	Oh, I'm sure that one had wings. Sometimes I think she's never quite left heaven, and never quite made it all the way here to earth. Maybe that's why she has such trouble staying here.

She hands the baby to MICHAEL.

NARRATION	Before she went away he held the baby for a while.
NARRATION	He touched her skin
NARRATION	And her tiny soft bones.
NARRATION	He felt the place where her wings had been.

MUM takes the baby, leaves for hospital.

NARRATION Then he went to Mina.

MICHAEL stands beneath MINA's tree.

MINA You're unhappy.

MICHAEL The baby's gone to hospital. Looks like she's going to bloody die.

MINA Die?

She jumps down from her tree.

MINA Would you like me to take you somewhere?

MICHAEL Somewhere?

MINA Somewhere secret. Five minutes. He won't even know you're gone! Come on. Quickly!

They leave the garden, hurry towards the DANGER house.

NARRATION At the end of the street she turned into another back lane.

NARRATION The houses behind the walls here were bigger and higher and older.

NARRATION	The back gardens were longer and had tall trees in them.
MINA	This is Crow Road.
NARRATION	She stopped outside a dark green gate.
NARRATION	She took a key from somewhere.
NARRATION	Unlocked the gate, slipped inside.

A cat brushes against MICHAEL's leg.

MINA	Whisper!
MICHAEL	What?
MINA	The cat's called Whisper. You'll see him everywhere.
NARRATION	She led him to a huge house with boards on all the windows.

There is a DANGER sign over the door.

MICHAEL	*DANGER!*
MINA	Take no notice. It's just to keep the vandals out. Come on. Quickly.

She unlocks the door, leads him in.

NARRATION	She led him through into the deep dark.
MICHAEL	Pitch black. Can't see.
MINA	Come on, Michael. Higher.
NARRATION	They ascended three stairways,
NARRATION	Passed three landings.
NARRATION	The stairs narrowed.
MINA	Don't stop. Keep going to the very top!
NARRATION	And they came to the final narrow doorway.
MINA	The attic. Stay very still in there. They might attack you.
MICHAEL	What might?
MINA	How brave are you? They know me and they know Whisper but they don't know you. How brave are you? As brave as me? You are! You have to be!

She leads MICHAEL through the attic door.

NARRATION	They were right inside the roof.

NARRATION Light came in through an arched window.

NARRATION They could see the rooftops and steeples of the town.

NARRATION The room darkened and reddened as the sun went down.

MINA Stay very still. Stay very quiet. Just watch.

MICHAEL Watch what?

MINA Just watch. Wait and watch. Look! Look!

NARRATION A pale bird rose from a corner and flew silently around the room.

NARRATION Then another came wheeling once around the room, its wings beating within inches of their faces before it too settled before the window.

NARRATION Michael didn't breathe.

NARRATION Mina gripped his hand.

NARRATION They watched the birds.

NARRATION The way their claws gripped the window frame.

NARRATION — The way their broad round faces turned to each other.

NARRATION — Then they went, flying silently out into the red dusk.

MICHAEL — Owls!

MINA — Tawny owls! Sometimes they'll attack intruders. But they knew you were with me. That's the nest. Don't go near. There's chicks in there. They'll defend them to the death. Come on. Quickly!

They leave the attic and run back to the garden.

MINA — Tell nobody.

MICHAEL — No.

MINA — Hope to die.

MICHAEL — What?

MINA — Cross your heart and hope to die.

MICHAEL — Cross my heart and hope to die.

MINA — Good.

They go to their separate homes.

NARRATION	He didn't go to school the next day.
NARRATION	He was having breakfast with Dad when he started trembling.
DAD	What about working with me in the garden today?

MICHAEL nods.

DAD	We'll get it all tidy for them, eh? You and me together.

DAD leads MICHAEL into the garden.

DAD	One day soon we'll have a pond over there.
MICHAEL	And a fountain.
DAD	Aye, and a bench.
MICHAEL	And a goal on the wall.
DAD	And a table for the nosh and the drinks.
MICHAEL	And a place where Mum can sunbathe.

DAD Somewhere for the baby's playpen.

MICHAEL And lovely soft grass for her.

DAD Aye. Of course we'll have to cover the pond once she's crawling.

MICHAEL Aye. Of course.

DAD Ha! And that damn death trap'll be long gone by then. Whack! Whack! It'll be great, son.

DAD goes into the house.

NARRATION Michael stood up and went to the garage door.

NARRATION He stood listening.

MICHAEL You can't just sit there! You can't just sit like you're waiting to die!

NARRATION There was no answer.

MICHAEL You can't!

NARRATION No answer.

DAD comes out.

DAD All right, son?

MICHAEL Aye.

DAD 27 and 53 again?

MICHAEL Aye.

DAD You can go round to the Chinese later.

NARRATION All that morning, they cleared a wider and wider space.

NARRATION They watched the blackbirds dig into the soil where they'd been working.

Mina appears in her garden.

DAD Hey, look. You can finish the garden tomorrow. Go on.

Go and see Mina.

Michael goes to Mina.

MINA You're not at school today.

MICHAEL I'm not well. The baby might not die.

MINA That's good.

MICHAEL You're not at school either.

MINA — I don't go to school. My mother educates me. We believe that schools inhibit the natural curiosity, creativity and intelligence of children. The mind needs to be opened out into the world, not shuttered down inside a gloomy classroom.

MICHAEL — Oh.

MINA — Don't you agree?

MICHAEL — Don't know.

MINA — Our motto is on the wall by my bed: "How can a bird that is born for joy/Sit in a cage and sing?" William Blake. The chicks in the nest won't need a classroom to make them fly. Will they?

MICHAEL — No.

MINA — Well then. My father believed this too.

MICHAEL — Your father?

MINA — Yes. He was a wonderful man. He died before I was born. We often think of him, watching us from heaven. You're a quiet person.

MICHAEL Do you believe we're descended from the apes?

MINA Not a matter of belief. It's a proven fact. It's called evolution. You must know that. Yes, we are. I would hope, though, that we also have some rather more beautiful ancestors.

MICHAEL It was great to see the owls.

MINA Yes. They're wild things, of course. Killers, savages. They're wonderful.

MICHAEL Cups his hands together.

MICHAEL Listen.

He blows between his hands, hoots like an owl.

MINA That's brilliant! Show me.

He shows her again.

MINA Brilliant. So brilliant!

MICHAEL Leakey showed me. My mate at school. There's something I could show you as well. Like you showed me the owls.

MINA What is it?

MICHAEL	I don't know. I don't even know if it's true or if it's a dream.
MINA	That's all right. Truth and dreams are always getting muddled.
MICHAEL	I'd have to take you there and show you.
MINA	Come on, then.
MICHAEL	Not now. Got to go and get 27 and 53.
MINA	Mystery man, that's you.
MICHAEL	Do you know what shoulder blades are for?
MINA	Do you not even know that?
MICHAEL	Do you?
MINA	It's a proven fact. Common knowledge. They're where your wings were, and where they'll grow again. Go on, then, mystery man. Go and get your mysterious numbers.

MICHAEL runs to the Chinese takeaway.

NARRATION	Spring roll, prawn cracker, special

chow mein, pork char sui, beef and mushroom, OK.

NARRATION Just before dawn, next morning.

MICHAEL gets the Chinese food out of the bin and goes to the garage. He switches on his torch, creeps inside, goes to Skellig.

SKELLIG You again.

MICHAEL More 27 and 53.

SKELLIG Food of the gods. Nectar.

MICHAEL How do you know about 27 and 53?

SKELLIG Ernie's favorite. Used to hear him on the phone. 27 and 53, he used to say. Bring it round. Bring it quick.

MICHAEL You were in the house?

SKELLIG In the garden. Watched him through the window. Found his leavings in the bin next morning. 27 and 53. Sweetest of nectars. Lovely change from spiders and mice.

MICHAEL Did he see you? Did he know you were there?

SKELLIG Never could tell. Used to look at me, but look right through me, like I wasn't there. Miserable old toot. Mebbe thought I was a figment. D'you think I'm a figment?

MICHAEL Don't know what you are.

SKELLIG That's all right, then.

MICHAEL Are you dead?

SKELLIG Ha!

MICHAEL Are you?

SKELLIG Yes! The dead are often known to eat 27 and 53 and to suffer from Arthur Itis.

MICHAEL You need more aspirin?

SKELLIG Not yet.

MICHAEL Anything else?

SKELLIG 27 and 53.

MICHAEL The baby's in hospital.

SKELLIG Some brown.

MICHAEL Brown?

SKELLIG Brown ale. Something else Ernie used to have. Something else he couldn't finish. Eyes bigger than his belly. Brown ale. Sweetest of nectars.

SKELLIG belches and retches. MICHAEL shines his torch onto the bulges on his shoulders. He reaches out to touch. SKELLIG flinches.

SKELLIG No. I said, no!

MICHAEL There's someone I'd like to bring to see you.

SKELLIG Someone to tell you I'm really here.

MICHAEL She's nice.

SKELLIG No.

MICHAEL She's clever.

SKELLIG Nobody.

MICHAEL She'll know how to help you.

SKELLIG Ha!

MICHAEL I don't know what to do. The garage is going to bloody collapse or they're going to pull it down. You're ill with bloody arthritis. You don't eat properly. The baby's ill and we hope she won't die but she might. She really might. My friend's nice. She'll tell nobody else. She's clever. She'll know how to help you.

SKELLIG Damn kids.

MICHAEL She's called Mina.

SKELLIG Bring the street. Bring the whole damn town.

MICHAEL Just Mina. And me.

SKELLIG Kids.

MICHAEL What shall I call you?

SKELLIG Eh?

MICHAEL What should I tell her you're called?

SKELLIG Mr. Nobody. Mr. Bones and Mr. Had Enough and Mr. Arthur Itis. Now get out and leave me alone.

MICHAEL OK.

MICHAEL starts to go.

MICHAEL — Will you think about the baby?

SKELLIG — Eh?

MICHAEL — Will you think about her in hospital? Will you think about her getting better? Please.

SKELLIG — Yes. Blinking yes. Yes. Yes, I will.

MICHAEL leaves the garage.

NARRATION — Outside, night had almost given way to day.

NARRATION — The blackbird was on the garage roof, belting out its song.

NARRATION — Black and pink and blue were mingling in the sky.

NARRATION — He looked into the sky and saw the owls heading homeward on great silent wings.

NARRATION — He seemed to see a face inside the darkness of an upstairs window in Mina's house.

MICHAEL puts his hands to his mouth and hoots.

Something answers: hoot, hoot, hoot.

NARRATION	The next morning, he was with Dad again working in the garden.
MICHAEL	Will the baby be back soon then?
DAD	A few days maybe. They need to keep an eye on her.
MICHAEL	She's coming on then?
DAD	Flying. That's what Doctor Bloom said, flying.
MICHAEL	Dad, can I go and see Mina again?
DAD	Don't worry about me. I'll do all the dirty work. You just run around and have a good time. Hey, Michael, you'd better be here tomorrow. I've got them coming to pull down the garage. You wouldn't want to miss that.

MICHAEL hurries to MINA's house.

NARRATION Mina's blanket and books were on the lawn, but Mina wasn't there.

NARRATION He looked up into the tree and she wasn't there.

NARRATION He stepped over the wall, went to the front door, rang the doorbell.

MRS. MCKEE comes to the door.

MICHAEL Is Mina in?

MRS. MCKEE She is. You must be Michael. I'm Mrs. McKee. *(She calls.)* Mina! How's the baby?

MICHAEL Very well. Well, we think she'll be very well.

MRS. MCKEE Babies are stubborn things. Strugglers and fighters. Tell your parents I'm thinking of them.

MICHAEL I will.

MINA appears at the door.

MINA We're modeling. Come and see.

MRS. MCKEE Mina's fixated on birds just now. Sometimes it's things that swim, sometimes it's things that slink through the night, sometimes it's things that creep and crawl, but just now it's things that fly.

NARRATION There were shelves full of clay models.

NARRATION Foxes,

NARRATION Fish,

NARRATION Lizards,

NARRATION Hedgehogs,

NARRATION Little mice,

NARRATION And then an owl.

MICHAEL Did you make all those? They're brilliant.

MINA shows him a clay bird.

MINA Once it's fired and glazed I'll hang it from the ceiling.

MRS. MCKEE Like magic, eh?

MICHAEL Like magic, yes.

MINA I've told him what we think of schools.

"To go to school on a summer morn,

O! It drives all joy away;

Under a cruel eye outworn,

The little ones spend the day

In sighing and dismay."

William Blake again. You've heard of William Blake?

MRS. MCKEE Mina!

MICHAEL No.

MINA He painted pictures and wrote poems. Much of the time he wore no clothes. He saw angels in his garden.

MRS. MCKEE Mina!

MICHAEL I was going for a walk.

MINA Can I go for a walk with Michael, Mum?

MRS. MCKEE Yes. But not too long or your clay'll dry out.

MICHAEL leads MINA towards the garage.

MINA Not at school again?

MICHAEL No.

MINA Good. Oh! Be quiet. Be very very quiet. Listen.

MICHAEL Listen to what?

MINA Just listen. What can you hear?

MICHAEL Traffic. Birds singing. Breeze in the trees.

MINA Listen closer. Listen harder.

MICHAEL My own heart! I can hear my own heart!

MINA That's nothing. Listen deeper. Listen for the tiniest sweetest noise.

MICHAEL What am I listening for?

MINA It comes from above you, from inside the tree.

MICHAEL Inside the tree?

MINA Just do it, Michael. It comes from the nest. Just listen.

MICHAEL Yes! The chicks!

MINA The chicks, Michael! You can hear the cheeping chicks.

MICHAEL continues to listen in amazement.

MINA Their bones are more delicate than ours. Their bones are almost hollow. Did you know that?

MICHAEL I think so.

MINA picks up a bone.

MINA From a pigeon, we believe. Feel how light it is. See how much air is inside. The presence of air cavities within the bone is known as pneumatization. This is the result of evolution. Over millions of years, the bird has developed an anatomy that enables it to fly. And we have not. You understand?

MICHAEL I think so.

MINA One day, I'll tell you about the archaeopteryx.

MINA cups her hands, makes the owl sound.

MINA Brilliant! Brilliant!

MICHAEL I made the hooting sound last night. Just after dawn, very early in the morning.

MINA Did you?

MICHAEL Were you looking out then? Did you make the owl sound then?

MINA I can't be certain.

MICHAEL Can't?

MINA I dream. I walk in my sleep. Sometimes I do things really and I think they're just dreams. Sometimes I dream them and think they're real. Don't you?

No answer.

MINA Don't you, Michael?

MICHAEL Yes.

MINA Good.

MICHAEL I told you there was something I could show you.

MINA Then show me.

MICHAEL Then come on!

NARRATION He led her quickly along the front street.

NARRATION He turned into the back lane.

NARRATION He led her past the high back garden walls.

MINA Where is it?

MICHAEL Not far. The place is filthy, and it's dangerous.

MINA Good! Don't stop, Michael!

NARRATION He led her to the garage.

MINA Here? Just here?

MICHAEL Yes. Yes.

He shows her some cod-liver oil capsules. He picks up a bottle of brown ale from just inside the garage door. He takes a torch from his pocket.

MICHAEL We'll need these. Trust me, Mina. I'm worried that you won't see what I think I see.

MINA I'll see whatever's there. Take me in.

They enter the garage.

MICHAEL Keep close, Mina.

NARRATION Things scratched and scuttled across the floor.

NARRATION Cobwebs snapped on their clothes and skin.

NARRATION The ceiling creaked.

NARRATION Michael trembled.

NARRATION Maybe Mina would see nothing.

NARRATION Maybe he'd been wrong all along.

NARRATION Maybe dreams and truth were just a useless muddle in his mind.

Michael shines the torch onto Skellig.

SKELLIG Again.

Mina recoils, stifles a cry. Michael holds her arm.

MICHAEL I brought my friend. Like I said I would. This is Mina.

Skellig turns his eyes to Mina. Is there a moment of recognition? Michael holds up the brown ale.

MICHAEL I brought this as well.

MICHAEL opens the bottle. He pours brown ale into SKELLIG's mouth.

SKELLIG Nectar. Drink of the gods.

MINA Who are you?

SKELLIG Mr. Had Enough of You.

MICHAEL helps him to drink again. He shows him the cod-liver oil capsules.

MICHAEL I brought these as well. People swear by them.

SKELLIG Stink of fish. Slimy slithery swimming things.

MICHAEL He just sits there. It's like he's waiting to die. I don't know what to do.

SKELLIG Do nothing.

MINA crouches beside SKELLIG, takes the torch, stares at him, touches him.

MINA Who are you?

SKELLIG Nobody.

MINA	Dry and cold. How long have you been here?
SKELLIG	Long enough.
MINA	Are you dead?
SKELLIG	Kids' questions. All the same.
MICHAEL	Tell her things. She's clever. She'll know what to do.
SKELLIG	Let me see her.
MINA	I'm called Mina. I'm Mina, you're . . .
SKELLIG	You're Mina. I'm sick to death.

Mina touches his hands, his skin.

MINA	Calcification. The process by which the bones harden and become inflexible. The process by which the body turns to stone.
SKELLIG	Not as stupid as she looks.
MINA	It is linked to another process, by which the mind, too, becomes inflexible. It stops thinking and

imagining. It becomes hard as bone. It is no longer a mind. It is a lump of bone wrapped in a wall of stone. This process is ossification.

SKELLIG More beer.

MICHAEL helps SKELLIG to drink.

SKELLIG Take her away.

MICHAEL guides MINA's hand to SKELLIG's shoulder blades.

NARRATION Michael took Mina's hand.

NARRATION He guided it towards the shoulder blades.

NARRATION He pressed her fingers to the growths beneath the jacket.

MINA What are you?

MICHAEL You've got to leave here. They're going to pull it all down. Tomorrow.

MINA We can help you. There's somewhere we could take you. It's safer there. You could just sit there dying too, if that's really what you want.

SKELLIG More beer.

MICHAEL	One of these as well.

MICHAEL helps SKELLIG to drink. He drops a cod-liver oil capsule onto SKELLIG's tongue. SKELLIG gags.

MINA	You have to let us help you.
NARRATION	The roof trembled in the breeze.
NARRATION	Dust continued to fall on them.
NARRATION	Tears fell from Michael's eyes.
MICHAEL	Please.
SKELLIG	Where did you come from?
MICHAEL	What?
SKELLIG	You. From.
MICHAEL	Me? There. Out there. Why?
SKELLIG	Go away.
MICHAEL	Why won't you move?

SKELLIG sighs.

SKELLIG	More beer.
MICHAEL	I hate you. I hate you!

MINA — You have to let us help.

SKELLIG — Do it. Do what you want.

MICHAEL — Tonight.

MICHAEL and MINA leave the garage. They stand outside.

MINA — He's an extraordinary being. What's on his back?

They stare and wonder and are silent. The blackbird sings.

MINA — We'll take him out tonight.

MICHAEL — At dawn.

MINA — We'll call to each other. We'll hoot like owls. We'll make sure we don't sleep. An extraordinary being.

MICHAEL — I'll go back to my dad now.

MINA — I'll go back to my clay.

MICHAEL — I'll see you at dawn.

MINA — At dawn. I won't sleep.

MICHAEL — I won't sleep.

Mina leaves.

MICHAEL He won't die. He won't just die.

Dad comes into the garden.

DAD You like Mina then?

Michael shrugs.

DAD You do.

MICHAEL She's . . . extraordinary.

Michael's room, night. The hooting of an owl.

NARRATION Michael slept.

NARRATION In his dream he was with the baby.

NARRATION They were tucked up together in the blackbird's nest.

MICHAEL Then I heard the owl and saw Mina in the wilderness.

Mina hoots.

NARRATION He tiptoed out of the house.

NARRATION Mina was waiting.

MICHAEL I didn't sleep all night. Then at the very last minute when the night was ending I did.

MINA But you're awake now?

MICHAEL Yes.

MINA We're not dreaming it?

MICHAEL We're not dreaming it.

MINA We're not dreaming it together?

MICHAEL Even if we were we wouldn't know.

The blackbird sings.

MINA Quickly, Michael. No time to waste.

MICHAEL and MINA enter the garage, move to SKELLIG.

MINA You have to come with us.

SKELLIG I'm sick to death.

MINA You have to come.

SKELLIG I'm weak as a baby.

MINA Babies aren't weak. Have you

seen a baby screaming for its food or struggling to crawl? Have you seen a blackbird chick daring its first flight?

Mina tries to lift him. Michael helps her.

MINA — Please.

SKELLIG — I'm frightened.

Mina kisses him on the cheek.

MINA — Don't be frightened. We're taking you to safety.

Skellig struggles to rise from the floor.

NARRATION — His joints creaked as he struggled to rise from the floor.

NARRATION — They felt how thin he was.

NARRATION — How extraordinarily light he was.

NARRATION — Their fingers touched behind his back.

NARRATION — They explored the growths upon his shoulder blades.

NARRATION — They felt them folded up like arms.

NARRATION — They stared into each other's eyes,

NARRATION And didn't dare to tell each other what they thought they felt.

MINA Extraordinary, extraordinary being.

MICHAEL Move slowly. Hold on to us.

They move out of the garage into the intensifying daylight.

NARRATION He turned his face away from the intensifying light.

NARRATION They saw for the first time that he wasn't old.

NARRATION He seemed like a young man.

MINA You're beautiful!

NARRATION Already traffic could be heard in the city.

NARRATION The birds in the gardens yelled their songs.

NARRATION Michael told himself,

MICHAEL This is a dream.

NARRATION He told himself,

MICHAEL Anything's possible in a dream. We'll carry him!

MINA	Yes!

They lift him.

MINA	You're so light. What are you?

SKELLIG groans.

NARRATION	They carried him into the back lane.
NARRATION	They turned into another lane.
NARRATION	They could hear the cars on nearby Crimdon Road.
NARRATION	They carried him to the green gate of the boarded house.
NARRATION	They hurried to the door with the red sign.
NARRATION	They went through the DANGER door.
NARRATION	They moved into the darkness.
NARRATION	And then into the first room.
NARRATION	They laid him there on the floor.
NARRATION	And for a time they paused.
NARRATION	As if exhausted.

NARRATION	As if they slept together there.
NARRATION	Inside the deep deep deepest dark.

MICHAEL gasps in surprise, as if suddenly waking.

MICHAEL	My dad! He'll wake up soon. I have to go back.
MINA	You're safe now.
SKELLIG	Knackered. Sick to death. Aspirin.

MICHAEL feeds SKELLIG aspirin.

MINA	We'll make you well now. Is there anything you need?
MICHAEL	27 and 53.
SKELLIG	27 and 53.

MINA kisses SKELLIG. She stretches her arms around his back.

MINA	What are you?

SKELLIG shakes his head. He begins to crawl away from her.

SKELLIG	Nothing. Nothing.
MINA	Let us help you. I'll make you more comfortable.

She begins to pull his jacket down over his shoulders.

NARRATION	She slid the jacket over his arms.
SKELLIG	No. No!
MINA	Trust me.
NARRATION	She took the jacket right off him.
NARRATION	They saw what both of them had dreamed they would see.
NARRATION	Beneath his jacket were wings that grew out through rips in his shirt.
NARRATION	The wings began to unfurl from his shoulder blades.
NARRATION	They were twisted and uneven.
NARRATION	They were covered in cracked and crooked feathers.
NARRATION	They clicked and trembled as they opened.
NARRATION	They were wider than his shoulders, higher than his head.
NARRATION	He whimpered with pain.

NARRATION	His tears fell.
NARRATION	They reached out to touch.
MINA	You're beautiful!
SKELLIG	Let me sleep. Let me go home.
NARRATION	His wings continued to quiver into life above him.
NARRATION	They touched them.
NARRATION	They felt the feathers,
NARRATION	And beneath them the bones and sinews and muscles that supported them.
NARRATION	They felt the trembling of his heart.
NARRATION	They felt the crackle of his breathing.
MINA	Oh, what are you?
MICHAEL	Who are you?
MINA	Who?
SKELLIG	My name is Skellig.

ACT TWO

The hospital. The baby is in a glass case.

NARRATION In hospital, the baby was in a glass case.

NARRATION There were wires and tubes in her.

NARRATION They looked down through the glass.

Mum, Dad and Michael stare down at her.

DAD She'll be home in a day or two. This is all routine.

MUM Look at her. Don't fly too far, little chick.

MUM You getting on all right, son? Dad's looking after you? Is there anything you need?

DAD 27 and 53.

MICHAEL Aye. 27 and 53. 27 and 53.

MUM Look, Michael. She's smiling. Can you see? Can you see?

NARRATION But it didn't look like a smile to him.

MUM You look so tired, love. You two been staying up late?

DAD — Dead right. It's been videos and Chinese takeaways every night. Hasn't it, son?

MICHAEL — Aye.

MICHAEL — Got to go out a minute, Mum.

NARRATION — He went out into the corridor.

MICHAEL meets a nurse.

MICHAEL — Excuse me.

NURSE — Yes?

MICHAEL — Do you know where the people with arthritis go?

NURSE — Straight to heaven, to make up for their pains on earth. Or Ward 34, love. Top floor. Silly place to put people with bad bones that's got trouble walking and climbing stairs. But who am I to know?

MICHAEL goes higher. He meets an old woman with a walker.

OLD WOMAN — Knackered! Once up and down the ward and three times round the landing. Absolutely knackered!

MICHAEL Arthritis.

OLD WOMAN That's right. Arthur. But I've got two new hips and I'll be dancing soon and that'll show him who's boss.

She jiggles in the walker as if dancing, then laughs.

OLD LADY Daft owld biddy!

MICHAEL I've got a friend with arthritis.

OLD WOMAN Poor soul.

MICHAEL What'll help him?

OLD WOMAN Some folk swear by cod-liver oil and a positive mind. For me, there's prayers to Our Lady, and Doctor McNabola with his plastic bits and pieces and his glue. Talk of the devil!

Dr. McNabola passes by. He is doing his daily rounds with a clutch of students.

OLD WOMAN Keep on moving. That's the thing. Don't let everything seize up.

Old woman shuffles off, humming "Lord of the Dance."

NARRATION He looked inside Ward 34.

NARRATION People were practicing moving on walkers.

NARRATION They were calling to each other across the ward.

NARRATION They were wincing,

NARRATION And gasping,

NARRATION And grinning.

MICHAEL Excuse me. Doctor McNabola.

Dr. McNabola stops, looks at Michael.

MICHAEL What's good for arthritis?

DR. MCNABOLA The needle. Deep injections right into the joint. Then the saw. The lovely sound of steel on bone. Bits cut out and new bits put in. Stitch it up, good as new. Are you a sufferer, young man?

MICHAEL A friend.

DR. MCNABOLA Tell your friend to come to me. I'll needle him, saw him, fix him up and send him home nearly as good as new. Failing that, the advice is simple. Keep cheerful. Take cod-liver oil. Remain active.

Most of all, don't give up. Anything else?

MICHAEL shakes his head.

DR. MCNABOLA Then I must carry on.

DR. MCNABOLA moves on.

OLD WOMAN He's a bighead, but he's right. Your friend needs a kick up the backside, eh?

MICHAEL nods.

OLD WOMAN So kick him up the bliddy backside. Make him dance.

MICHAEL hurries back to MUM, DAD and the baby. MUM has been crying.

MUM You've been a while.

DAD Too much 27, eh?

MUM Cod-liver oil. That'll sort you out.

MUM reaches out for MICHAEL, holds him.

MUM You can put your hand through the holes in the side to touch her.

MICHAEL reaches in to touch the baby.

MUM	That's right. Let her know you're here. Tell her your name.
MICHAEL	I'm Michael. I'm your big brother.
MUM	Tell her you love her. Go on, son. Love's the thing that'll make her better.
MICHAEL	I love you. I love you.
NARRATION	He listened deeper,
NARRATION	Until he heard the baby,
NARRATION	The gentle squeaking of her breath,
NARRATION	Tiny and distant, as if it came from a different world.
NARRATION	He listened until he heard her beating heart.
NARRATION	He told himself,
MICHAEL	If I listen hard enough, her breath and her heart will never be able to stop.

MICHAEL holds his heart, backs away.

MUM	You're my best boy. Whatever happens, you'll always be my best boy.

NARRATION And he went to Mina, once again.

Mina's garden. Michael and Mina sit beneath the tree. Mina has a heavy encyclopedia. She has a clay model of the archaeopteryx that she guides through the air as she talks. Michael holds his heart as he listens.

MINA Here it is. Archaeopteryx. The dinosaur that flew. We believe that dinosaurs became extinct. But there's another theory, that their descendants are with us still. The little archaeopteryx survived, and began the line of evolution that led to birds. Wings and feathers, see? But the creature was a heavy, bony thing capable of nothing but short, sudden flights. From tree to tree, stone to stone.

She imitates the archaeopteryx's thump to earth.

MINA It couldn't rise and spiral and dance like birds can now.

She imitates a bird's spiraling flight.

The blackbird sings nearby.

MINA	If you held the true archaeopteryx, it would be almost as heavy as stone in your hands. There is no end to evolution, Michael. Maybe this is not how we are meant to be forever.
MICHAEL	Mina.
MINA	Yes.
MICHAEL	I can feel the baby's heart inside my own.
MINA	Inside?
MICHAEL	It's beating beside mine. And I feel her breathing along with me. Feel it, Mina.

Mina feels his heart.

MICHAEL	Can you feel? There. And there. And there.
MINA	Yes. No. Yes!
MICHAEL	If I can feel it beating there beside my own, I know the baby's safe. You feel it?
MINA	Yes.

They concentrate together.

MINA Yes. Extraordinary. *We* are extraordinary.

MICHAEL/MINA Skellig! Skellig! Skellig!

MICHAEL Extraordinary.

MICHAEL and MINA look deep into each other's eyes, lost in the wonder of themselves and of SKELLIG.

Then LEAKEY and COOT arrive, and giggle down at them.

LEAKEY/COOT Ahahahahahaha!

NARRATION Then Leaky and Coot came over.

LEAKEY/COOT Ahahahahahaha!

LEAKEY Howay, man, Michael!

They play football. MINA retreats, watches from her tree.

COOT On me head! On me head!

NARRATION Michael was hopeless.

LEAKEY On me head! On me head!

COOT Michael, man! What's wrong with you, man?

LEAKEY It's cos he's been ill.

COOT Bollocks. He's not been ill, he's just been upset.

MICHAEL I'm out of practice.

COOT Bollocks.

LEAKEY That's right.

COOT It's her. Her in the tree. That lass he was with.

LEAKEY That's right.

MICHAEL Bollocks.

LEAKEY It's that lass.

COOT That lass that climbs in a tree like a monkey. Her that sits in a tree like a crow.

MICHAEL Bollocks.

LEAKEY He holds hands with her.

COOT She says he's extraordinary.

LEAKEY Extraordinary!

MICHAEL Get stuffed.

MICHAEL moves away from them. LEAKEY and COOT follow.

MICHAEL The baby's ill. Really ill. The doctor says I'm in distress.

LEAKEY Yeah. Yeah, I know. I'm sorry.

LEAKEY Who is she, anyway?

MICHAEL She's called Mina.

LEAKEY What school's she at?

MICHAEL She doesn't go to school.

LEAKEY Plays the wag, eh?

COOT Or is she just too thick?

MICHAEL Her mother teaches her.

LEAKEY Hell's teeth. Thought you had to go to school. Lucky sod.

COOT What'll she do for mates, though? And who'd like to be stuck at home all day?

MICHAEL They think schools stop you from learning. They think schools try to make everybody just the same.

COOT That's bollocks, that.

LEAKEY Aye. You're learning all day long in school.

MICHAEL Maybe.

LEAKEY Is that why you've not been coming in? Is it cos you're never coming back again? You're going to let that lass's mother teach you?

MICHAEL Course not. But they're going to teach me some things.

LEAKEY Like?

MICHAEL Like modeling with clay. And about William Blake.

COOT Who's he? That bloke that's got the butcher's shop in town?

MICHAEL He said school drives all joy away. He was a painter and a poet.

COOT Oh, aye?

LEAKEY Oh, aye?

MICHAEL Look. I can't tell you everything. But the world's full of amazing things. I've seen them.

Coot catches sight of Mina.

COOT There she is.

LEAKEY The girl in the tree.

COOT Hey. Mebbe Rasputin's right about that evolution stuff. He could come and look at her and see there's monkeys all around us still.

Leakey and Coot run off, laughing.

MINA "Thank God I was never sent to school,
To be flog'd into following the style of a Fool."

MICHAEL You know nothing about it. We don't get flogged and my friends aren't fools.

MINA Ha!

MICHAEL You know nothing about it. You might know about William Blake, but you know nothing about what ordinary people do.

MINA — Ha!

MICHAEL — Yes. Ha!

MINA — They hate me. I could see it in their eyes. They think I'm taking you away from them. They're stupid.

MICHAEL — They're not stupid!

MINA — Stupid. Kicking balls and jumping at each other and screeching like hyenas. Stupid. Yes, hyenas! You as well.

MICHAEL — Hyenas? They think you're a monkey, then.

MINA — See what I mean? They know nothing about me but they hate me.

MICHAEL — And of course you know everything about them.

MINA — There's nothing to know. Kicking, screeching, being stupid.

MICHAEL — Ha!

MINA — Yes, ha! And that little ginger one . . .

MICHAEL — Blake was little and ginger.

MINA	How do you know that?
MICHAEL	See? You think nobody but you can know anything.
MINA	No, I don't.
MICHAEL	Ha!
MINA	Go home. Go and play stupid football or something. Leave me alone.

Michael runs from her. He plays football alone with a desperate energy.

Dad appears.

DAD	Michael. Michael!

Michael looks at him, doesn't respond.

DAD	You can tell me, son. Come on, eh?
MICHAEL	Leave me alone! There's nothing to tell. There's nothing to bloody tell!

Night. Michael's bedroom. The hooting of owls. Michael wakes, dresses, leaves.

NARRATION	The moon hung over the city.
NARRATION	He went out into the dark.
NARRATION	He walked through the deep shadows towards the DANGER house.

He finds MINA on the doorstep.

MINA	What took so long? Thought I was going to have to do this all alone.
MICHAEL	Thought that was what you wanted.
MINA	Oh, Michael. We said stupid things. I said stupid things.

An owl hoots.

MINA	Don't be angry. Be my friend.
MICHAEL	I am your friend.
MINA	It's possible to hate your friend. You hated me today.
MICHAEL	You hated me.
MINA	I love the night. Anything seems possible at night when the rest of the world has gone to sleep. Oh, Michael, let's go inside.

MICHAEL — Yes, let's go inside.

NARRATION — So they stepped again through the DANGER door.

They enter the house.

NARRATION — They blundered through the dark.

NARRATION — They found nothing.

MINA — Where is he?

MICHAEL — Skellig!

MINA — Skellig!

NARRATION — No answer.

NARRATION — Their hearts thundered.

MICHAEL — Where is he?

NARRATION — They stumbled up the stairs.

MICHAEL — Skellig!

MINA — Skellig!

NARRATION — No answer.

MINA — Stand still. Listen to the deepest deepest places of the dark.

NARRATION	They held hands.
NARRATION	They listened to the night.
NARRATION	Michael heard the breathing of the baby deep inside himself.
NARRATION	He heard the far-off beating of her heart.
NARRATION	They listened to the dark.
MINA	You hear?
MICHAEL	Yes!
MINA	Skellig's breathing!
MICHAEL	He's up there.
NARRATION	They climbed the final flight of stairs
NARRATION	Towards the final doorway.
NARRATION	Gently, fearfully, they opened the door.
NARRATION	They saw his silhouette against the arched window.
NARRATION	They didn't dare move.

NARRATION	And as they watched, an owl appeared,
NARRATION	Dropping on silent wings from the moonlit sky to the moonlit window.
NARRATION	It laid something on the windowsill,
NARRATION	And flew off again.
NARRATION	Skellig bent his head to where the bird had been,
NARRATION	And he ate the thing that had been left there.
MINA	They're feeding him!
NARRATION	And then he turned to them.
SKELLIG	Come to me.

They don't move.

SKELLIG	Come to me.

They go to him. He takes their hands.

SKELLIG	Take my hand.

They make a circle.

NARRATION Michael caught the stench of Skellig's breath.

NARRATION His breath was the breath of an animal that lives on the meat of other living things.

NARRATION A dog.

NARRATION A fox.

NARRATION A blackbird.

NARRATION An owl.

NARRATION He stepped sideways and they turned together,

NARRATION And kept slowly turning,

NARRATION As if they were carefully, nervously,

NARRATION Beginning to dance.

They turn. Michael holds back.

SKELLIG Don't stop, Michael.

MINA No, Michael. Don't stop!

NARRATION He didn't stop.

NARRATION He felt Skellig's and Mina's hearts beating alongside his own.

NARRATION He felt their breath in rhythm with his.

NARRATION It was as if they moved into each other.

NARRATION As if they became one thing.

NARRATION And for a moment he saw ghostly wings at Mina's back.

NARRATION He felt feathers and delicate bones rising from his own shoulders.

NARRATION And he was lifted from the floor with Skellig and Mina.

NARRATION They turned circles together through the empty air of that empty room,

NARRATION High in an old house in Crow Road.

NARRATION And then it was over.

They return to the floor. SKELLIG *touches the children's heads.*

SKELLIG Go home now.

MICHAEL But how are you like this now?

SKELLIG The owls and the angels. Remember this night. Remember this night.

MICHAEL and MINA retreat.

MICHAEL Did it happen to you as well?

MINA Yes, it happened to all of us.

NARRATION They stepped back out together into the night.

MINA It will happen again, won't it?

MICHAEL Yes.

NARRATION They hurried homeward, filled with joy.

DAD appears.

DAD Michael! Michael! What do you think you're doing, man?

MINA We were sleepwalking.

MICHAEL Yes, I was sleepwalking.

MINA goes.

DAD It's school for you tomorrow!

School bell rings.

In the classroom.

RASPUTIN has a long poster of a cut-away person: lungs, heart, etc., all exposed.

RASPUTIN Here we are. Our dark interior.

He beckons COOT towards him, acts out stripping away COOT's skin, tearing open his chest.

RASPUTIN Come here, Mr. Coot. Now, this is what we would see were we to open up Mr. Coot. Lungs, stomach, intestines, a network of blood vessels and nerves. The bones, the brain and then, of course, the heart. This is what all of our evolution has been leading to. The inner us.

COOT Ugh!

RASPUTIN Yes, Mr. Coot. Even the inner you.

RASPUTIN Yes. Inside we're all the same, no matter how horrible the outside might be.

COOT scuttles back to his desk.

RASPUTIN Now, I'd like you to place your hand on your chest like this. Feel the beating of your heart. This is our engine, beating day and night. Mostly we're hardly aware that it's even there. But if it stopped . . .

COOT squawks and pretends to die.

RASPUTIN Correct, Mr. Coot.

RASPUTIN too flops across his desk as if dead. Others copy. MICHAEL holds his heart, looks around him in fright.

School bell rings.

Break time. A game of football. MICHAEL plays with a desperate energy.

MICHAEL On me head! On me head! Yeah!

LEAKEY Give it to Michael! Go on!

COOT Look at him!

LEAKEY He's even better than he was before!

COOT You're OK again, Michael!

MICHAEL On me head! On me head! On me bloody head!

An English lesson with Miss Clarts. *She has been reading a story by* Michael.

MISS CLARTS Oh, Michael, your style is really coming on. And such an imagination.

She addresses the class, recounts Michael*'s story.*

MISS CLARTS A boy finds an old stinking tramp in a warehouse by the river who turns out to have wings under his ancient coat. The boy feeds the man with sandwiches and chocolate and the man becomes strong again. The man teaches the boy and his friend Kara how to fly. How do you come up with such things, Michael?

Rasputin *cuts in.*

RASPUTIN Michael. Could you come with me, please? Your dad's on the phone, Michael. He's been called to the hospital.

MICHAEL I should have stayed at home. I should have kept on thinking about her.

Michael *backs away.*

MISS CLARTS Michael?

RASPUTIN Michael?

Michael takes the phone.

MICHAEL Dad? Tomorrow? What do you mean, tomorrow? Operate? What they going to do? Dad, what are they going to do?

Michael drops the phone.

MICHAEL Her heart. They're operating on her heart.

NARRATION That night was endless.

NARRATION In and out of sleep.

NARRATION In and out of dreadful dreams.

NARRATION Deep in the night he left his bed.

NARRATION He went alone through the DANGER door.

NARRATION He went alone to Skellig.

Michael enters the DANGER *house.*

SKELLIG Michael. Did you bring me . . . ?

MICHAEL Nothing.

SKELLIG picks something from the floor and eats.

SKELLIG No Mina?

MICHAEL shakes his head.

NARRATION Michael moved closer.

SKELLIG What do you want?

NARRATION He smelt the stench.

NARRATION He touched the wings.

SKELLIG What do you want?

NARRATION There was no answer.

NARRATION Michael reached out.

SKELLIG No.

NARRATION He pressed his hand to Skellig's heart.

SKELLIG No.

MICHAEL Have you been thinking about her?

SKELLIG About who?

MICHAEL My sister.

NARRATION No answer.

MICHAEL She's going to die.

NARRATION No answer.

MICHAEL Skellig, man!

SKELLIG I'm tired. Leave me alone.

MICHAEL She's going to bloody die. What you going to do?

SKELLIG You don't know what you're saying.

MICHAEL I've given you everything, Skellig.

Skellig recoils.

MICHAEL You could do something. I know you could.

NARRATION But Skellig turned away.

SKELLIG Leave me alone.

MICHAEL She's tiny. She's weak. She's ill. She hasn't even got a name.

SKELLIG Get off me.

MICHAEL But she's braver than you are.

SKELLIG Oh, Michael.

MICHAEL You're just scared.

SKELLIG Go away. Go away.

MICHAEL There's nothing there.

SKELLIG Leave me alone. Go.

MICHAEL There's nothing. There's nowt. Nowt. Nowt.

NARRATION And Michael left.

NARRATION And closed the door on Skellig.

NARRATION Stumbled out into the dark.

NARRATION And woke to daylight with stinging eyes and sunken heart.

Dad and Michael in the kitchen.

MICHAEL No! I won't go to school! Why should I? Not today!

DAD You'll do as you're bloody told. You'll do what's best for your mum and the baby.

MICHAEL You just want me out of the way so you don't have to think about me and don't have to worry about me and you can just think about the bloody baby!

DAD Don't say bloody!

MICHAEL It is bloody! It's bloody bloody bloody! And it isn't fair!

Dad kicks the table.

DAD See? See the state you get me in? Go to bloody school!

Get out my bloody sight! I love you. I love you.

They hold each other.

DAD You could come, Michael. But there'd be nothing you could do. We just have to wait and pray. After school, go to Mina's for your tea. I'll come to get you when the operation's over. Keep believing.

Mina's house. Mina and Michael at the kitchen table with paints and paper. Mrs. McKee is preparing food. Mina has drawn a large picture of Skellig.

MRS. MCKEE It's lovely, isn't it, Michael?

MICHAEL Yes.

MRS. MCKEE The kind of thing William Blake saw. He said we were surrounded by angels and spirits. We must just open our eyes a little wider, look a little harder. But it's enough for me to have you two angels at my table. Isn't it amazing? I see you clearly, two angels at my table.

Michael and Mina draw. Mrs. McKee sings

MRS. MCKEE *(sings) I dreamt a dream! What can it mean?*
And that I was a maiden Queen . . .

MINA I went to Skellig today.

MRS. MCKEE *(sings) Guarded by an Angel mild*

Witless woe, was ne'er beguiled!

MICHAEL On your own?

MINA Yes. Skellig said, "Where's Michael?"

"At school," I said. "School!" he said. "He abandons me for school?" I said you hadn't abandoned him. I said you loved him.

MICHAEL I do.

MINA He says you must keep coming to see him. He says he's going away soon, Michael.

MRS. MCKEE *(sings) So he took his wings and fled: Then the morn blush'd rosy red . . .*

MICHAEL Going away?

MINA Yes.

MICHAEL Where to?

MINA He wouldn't say.

MICHAEL When?

MINA Soon.

MICHAEL Soon.

MRS. McKEE *(sings) Soon my Angel came again;*
I was armed, he came in vain,
For the time of youth was fled,
And gray hairs were on my head.

(speaks) Look. The fledglings are out.

She points into the garden.

MINA Come and see.

The blackbird calls its warning sound.

MINA Stay dead still and dead quiet. Look. Little brown feathered balls. Can you see them?

MICHAEL No. Yes!

MINA They're so exposed. So all alone. They're out of the nest. They can't fly. Their parents still have to feed them. All they can do is totter and tremble and hide in the shadows and wait for their food. They're in such peril. They'll be doing this all day. Flying and feeding all the way till dusk. And the same thing tomorrow and tomorrow till they can fly. Cats want them. And crows. And stupid dogs. They're so exposed, and death is all around.

MRS. MCKEE comes to MICHAEL and MINA. She's carrying a pomegranate in quarters. She passes them around, with pins to pick out the seeds.

MRS. MCKEE Thought you might like some of this.

MINA Pomegranates. Lovely.

MRS. MCKEE Pomegranate. Isn't it a lovely word? Look at all the life in it. Every pip could become a tree and every tree could bear a thousand fruits. It's what Persephone ate when she was waiting in the Underworld.

MICHAEL Who's Persephone?

MRS. MCKEE The goddess of the spring. She is forced to spend half the year in darkness deep underground. It's winter then—the days are cold and short and dark. Living things hide themselves away. Then she's released. She makes her slow way back up to the world again. The world gets brighter and bolder to welcome her back. Light and heat. Living things sense her approach. The animals dare to wake. Plants send out buds and shoots. Life dares to come back again. Spring comes back to the world.

MICHAEL An old myth. A story for ancient people and for little kids.

MRS. MCKEE But maybe it's a myth that's nearly true. Look around you, Michael. Fledglings, blooms, bright sunshine. Maybe what we see around us is the whole world welcoming Persephone home. They can do marvelous things, Michael. Maybe you'll soon be welcoming your own Persephone home.

They dream of Persephone's slow and perilous journey back towards the surface of the world.

MRS. MCKEE I'll watch the birds. Why not go and wander for a while?

Michael and Mina walk.

NARRATION It was like walking in a dream.

NARRATION The sun glared over the rooftops.

NARRATION Birds were ragged and black against the astonishing sky.

NARRATION The roadway glistened, a deep black pond.

MINA He'll be waiting for us, Michael. He'll be so pleased to see you.

NARRATION They entered in silence.

NARRATION	They went up in silence.
NARRATION	She led him into the attic.
MINA	Not here! Skellig! Skellig!
MICHAEL	Skellig!
NARRATION	He wasn't there.
MINA	He isn't here at all.

MICHAEL clutches his heart.

MICHAEL	Oh, Mina!
MINA	What is it?
MICHAEL	My heart's stopped. Feel my heart. There's nothing there.

He faints, falls.

MINA	Michael!

MINA touches his heart.

MINA	I can feel it. There and there and there.
MICHAEL	But it's only my heart. It's not the baby's.

MINA — Oh, Michael.

MICHAEL — It's only mine. Not the baby's. The baby's dead.

MINA — You can't know for certain.

MICHAEL — She's dead. Where is he? Skellig! Skellig! Where the hell are you? Skellig!

MINA — Don't, Michael.

MICHAEL — Maybe he's gone away forever, like he said he would. Maybe he was never even here at all!

MINA — Skellig! Skellig! Bloody Skellig!

DAD calls from outside.

DAD — Michael! Michael! Michael!

MINA — Come on, Michael.

MICHAEL doesn't move.

MINA — Come on.

They leave the house. They meet DAD outside.

DAD — It's over, son.

NARRATION Michael was wrong.

NARRATION She wasn't dead.

NARRATION She was snoring gently.

NARRATION Her little hands were clenched beside her head.

The hospital. DAD, MUM *and* MICHAEL *around the baby. A machine bleeps in rhythm with her heart.*

MUM They said she has a heart of fire. They said there was a moment when they thought they'd lost her. But she burst into life again. Wouldn't give in.

DAD We haven't even named her yet.

MICHAEL Persephone.

DAD Bit of a mouthful, eh?

MUM It was the strangest thing.

DAD What was?

MUM Well, I was lying here last night, tossing and turning. Kept getting up

	to look at her. Kept dropping off to sleep. And the strangest of dreams . . .
DAD	And . . . ?
MUM	And I saw this man. Another dream, though I was sure I was wide awake. He was standing over the baby. He was filthy. All in black, an ancient dusty suit. A great hunch on his back. Hair all matted and tangled. I was terrified. I wanted to reach out to him. I wanted to push him away. I wanted to scream, Get away from our baby! I wanted to shout for the nurses and doctors. But I couldn't move, couldn't speak, and I was sure he was going to take her away. But then he turned and looked at me. His face as dry and white as chalk. And such tenderness in his eyes. And for some reason I knew he hadn't come to harm her. I knew it would be all right. . . .
DAD	And . . . ?
MUM	And then he reached right down with both hands and lifted her up. She was wide awake. They stared

and stared into each other's eyes. He started to slowly turn around . . .

MICHAEL Like they were dancing.

MUM That's right. Like they were dancing. And then the strangest thing of all . . . The strangest thing of all, there were wings on the baby's back. Not solid wings. Transparent, ghostly, hardly visible, but there they were. Little feathery things. It looked so funny. The strange tall man and the little baby and the wings. And that was it. He put her back down, he turned and looked at me again and it was over. I slept like a log the rest of the night. When I woke they were already getting her ready for the operation. But I wasn't worried anymore. I kissed her and whispered to her how much we all loved her and they took her away. I knew it was going to be all right.

DAD And it is.

MUM And it is. I must have been thinking about what you asked me. What are shoulder blades for? Eh?

MICHAEL Yes. Yes.

MUM It isn't over. You know that, don't you? We'll have to protect her always, especially at first.

MICHAEL I know that. We'll love her and love her and love her.

DAD and MICHAEL prepare to leave.

MICHAEL See you tomorrow, Mum. See you tomorrow, little chick.

As they leave, MICHAEL sees DR. MCNABOLA with a clutch of students around him. MICHAEL hurries to him.

MICHAEL Doctor McNabola.

DR. MCNABOLA Yes.

MICHAEL I told you about my friend. The one with arthritis.

DR. MCNABOLA Aha! So is he ready for my needles and saw?

MICHAEL He seems to be getting better.

DR. MCNABOLA Splendid. Maybe he'll escape me yet.

MICHAEL Doctor?

DR. MCNABOLA Yes?

MICHAEL Can love help a person to get better?

DR. MCNABOLA Love. What can we doctors know about love? "Love is the child that breathes our breath, Love is the child that scatters death."

MICHAEL William Blake?

DR. MCNABOLA We have an educated man before us. Tell your friend that I hope he and I never have to meet.

Dr. McNabola moves on. Michael goes back to Dad.

DAD What was that all about?

MICHAEL Just somebody I met soon after the baby came in.

DAD Mystery man, that's you. She's not out of danger yet. You understand that, don't you?

MICHAEL Yes. But she will be, won't she?

DAD Yes! Yes, she blinking will! Hey, I know. We could have 27 and 53 tonight, eh?

MICHAEL 27 and 53. Sweetest of nectars.

DAD Sweetest of nectars. I like that. Sweetest of blinking nectars!

Michael and Mina enter the danger house.

NARRATION They went once more through the DANGER door.

NARRATION Once more into the attic.

NARRATION It was empty, dark and silent.

NARRATION They took 27 and 53 and brown ale.

NARRATION But there was no Skellig.

MINA He isn't here at all. Ah, well.

MICHAEL Feel my heart, Mina. Can you feel it? Her heart beating right inside there beside my own.

Mina touches his heart.

MICHAEL It's like touching and listening and imagining all at the same time. It's like blackbird chicks cheeping in a nest.

MINA Yes. Yes, there it is. There and there and there.

MICHAEL The baby's heart. It won't stop now.

MINA It won't stop now. I could sleep here. Just like this. And be happy forever.

MICHAEL Yes. But we have to go.

NARRATION They didn't move.

NARRATION And there came a rustling in the air outside.

NARRATION The stars were blocked out.

NARRATION The window creaked.

NARRATION And there he was, climbing in through the arched window.

MICHAEL Skellig.

SKELLIG Michael. Mina.

MICHAEL We brought you this, Skellig. 27 and 53.

SKELLIG Ha!

They crouch at his side and hold out the food. He slurps and licks and groans.

SKELLIG Sweetest of nectars. Food of the blinking gods.

MICHAEL And this.

He snaps the top off the brown ale and gives it to SKELLIG. He drinks.

SKELLIG Thought it was cold mice for supper and I come home to a banquet. Pair of angels, that's what you are.

MICHAEL You went to my sister.

SKELLIG Hm! Lovely thing.

MICHAEL You made her strong.

SKELLIG That one's glittering with life. Heart like fire. It was her that gave the strength to me. But worn out now. Knackered.

He touches MINA's and MICHAEL's faces.

SKELLIG But I'm getting strong, thanks to the angels and the owls.

MICHAEL You're going away.

SKELLIG nods.

MICHAEL Where will you go?

SKELLIG — Somewhere.

MICHAEL touches him.

MICHAEL — What are you, Skellig?

SKELLIG — Something. Something like you, something like a beast, something like a bird, something like an angel. Something like that. Let's stand up.

They make a circle, holding hands.

NARRATION — They made their circle.

NARRATION — They looked deep into each other's eyes.

NARRATION — And they held each other tight.

NARRATION — Their hearts beat as one.

NARRATION — They breathed as one.

NARRATION — They danced.

NARRATION — They turned once more in the empty air.

NARRATION — And ghostly wings rose from Michael's and Mina's backs.

NARRATION — And then it ended, and they came to earth again.

MINA	We'll remember forever.

Skellig hugs them both.

SKELLIG	Thank you for 27 and 53. Thank you for giving me my life again. Now you have to go home.
NARRATION	And so they left the attic.
NARRATION	And went down through the DANGER house.
NARRATION	And they stepped together into the astounding night.

At home.

NARRATION	It was really spring at last.
NARRATION	On a bright morning, the baby with the mended heart was carried from the hospital,
NARRATION	And she was brought back home to Falconer Road.
NARRATION	And her Mum and her Dad and her brother, Michael, sat around her,

NARRATION And looked at her in wonder.

NARRATION They laughed and laughed,

NARRATION And cried and cried,

NARRATION And they asked themselves,

DAD So, what shall we call her?

MUM Joy.

DAD Eh?

MUM Joy. We'll call her Joy.

Turn the book
over to read
Wild Girl,
Wild Boy.

Turn the book over to read *Skellig.*

WILD GIRL
Wild Boy

ALSO BY DAVID ALMOND

Skellig

Kit's Wilderness

Heaven Eyes

Counting Stars

Secret Heart

The Fire-Eaters

Skellig–The Play

DAVID ALMOND

WILD GIRL
WILD BOY

A PLAY

Delacorte Press

PREFACE

This is the tale of Elaine Grew, a brave and troubled young soul. She lives with her mother in an estate on the edge of a northern city. Outside the estate are an open hillside, a group of allotments, a lark-filled sky. Elaine has been happy here, but last year her dad died and now Elaine's in turmoil. She can't think straight, she can't see straight, she can't read or write. She squabbles and fights with her mother, who fears that Elaine is losing her mind, that she's losing touch with the world. Elaine's neighbors and schoolmates turn away from her. They mock her and scorn her and even fear her. Her teachers don't know what to do with her.

Elaine begins to stay away from school. She spends day after day in the wilderness of her dad's old allotment. She crawls like a lizard on the earth as she used to when he was with her. She slithers like a snake through the thorns and weeds. She works spells with spiders and digs in the earth for magic seeds.

What is she searching for? What will she find in the overgrown allotment, this place of memories, dreams and enchantment? And who is this wild boy who watches her and begins to move towards her?

For Mike Dalton

Wild Girl, Wild Boy

was commissioned by the Lyric Theatre, Hammersmith, and the Pop-Up Theatre company.

The play was first performed at the Lyric Theatre, Hammersmith, London, on 10 February 2001 in association with the Pop-Up Theatre company, directed by Michael Dalton, with the following cast:

JANET BAMFORD—Elaine
MARK HUCKETT—McNamara/Doctor
ANDREW OLIVER—Wild Boy/Father
MANDY VERNON-SMITH—Mother

DIRECTOR—Michael Dalton
ASSISTANT DIRECTOR—Jane Wolfson
DESIGNER—Will Hargreaves
MUSIC—Ransom Notes
CO-MUSICAL DIRECTORS—James Hesford, Mark Pearson
LIGHTING DESIGNER—Ace McCarron
COMPANY STAGE MANAGER—Emma Barron
SET CONSTRUCTION—Set Up Scenery
DIALECT COACH—Majella Hurley

The play received a Sainsbury's Checkout Theatre Award.

Characters

Elaine Grew, *a girl*

Elaine's mother

Elaine's father

Mr. McNamara, *a neighbor*

The Wild Boy, *also called Skoosh*

A doctor

A chorus of voices *These are the voices of schoolmates, teachers, neighbors. These voices provide a cruel commentary that echoes inside Elaine's head.*

SCENE ONE

Elaine's bedroom. Daytime. Bright blue sky is visible through the window. There are an untidy bed, a table, a chair. She is at a table, trying to write. On the table are pens and pencils, paper and notebooks. There are sheets of drawings, paintings and scribblings scattered on the table and floor. Pictures of birds and animals are pinned to the wall. A shelf on the wall holds pots of paints. Elaine's canvas shoulder bag hangs from her chair.

ELAINE — Wild . . . Girl . . . Wild . . . Boy . . .

That's the title. Good. That's the title.

Once . . . there . . . was . . . a . . . girl . . . called . . . Elaine . . .

Ah. Yes. Phew. That's the start . . .

She . . . lived . . . with . . .

She holds up the paper and looks at her words.

ELAINE — Look at it! Look at it! I'm so stupid. No, I'm not! I have problems . . . writing.

Something to do with the way I . . . see or something.

She looks around, peers into space, as if she's searching for something.

ELAINE Wild Boy? Wild Boy?

He's gone.

He was here, and now he's gone.

She goes to the window and peers out.

ELAINE Wild Boy! Where are you? Skoooooooosh! He was here, and now he's gone.

She rattles the window, rattles the door.

ELAINE Let me out! Let me out!

MUM (*from outside the room*)

Elaine! Elaine, just calm down, love!

ELAINE Let me out!

MUM Oh, Elaine. Be a good girl, will you?

ELAINE Ha, a good girl. That's my mum.

She doesn't understand. She doesn't see.

She's locked me in. Let me out!

SCENE ONE

ELAINE writes again.

ELAINE She lived with . . . Agh! Words on me fingers and on stupid paper slither and crawl and slip and slide and stagger like wounded things. Look at them. But words on me tongue can dance and sing like larky birds. So I'll tell it to you in dancing words and show it to you in moving pictures. And I'll tell it to me rattle as well. This is me rattle I've had since I was small.

ELAINE takes a big seedhead out of her canvas bag.

ELAINE A seedhead. A present from me dad. Rattle, rattle. Rattle, rattle. You'll wake the dead, me mum used to say. You'll bring the house down, girl. But she used to sing to it as well. And Dad was there then, and we were so happy! You should have seen the way we went on—specially me and Dad. The way we danced! We were so happy!

ELAINE shakes the seedhead. She dances. The sound and the dance lead her back into the past, into her memories, into the allotment. At moments like this, her bedroom and her dad's allotment merge.

MUM and DAD enter.

DAD comes to ELAINE and joins in with her dance.

MUM You two! I don't know what I'll do with you. You're daft as each other!

DAD holds some raspberries in his open hands. He holds out a raspberry towards ELAINE's mouth.

DAD Look at this, love. Taste it. It's from deep in the heart of the garden, deep in the thorns.

ELAINE It's a raspberry!

ELAINE takes the raspberry, eats it.

DAD A raspberry. Delicious and wild.

Oh, watch the juice! Lick it off!

They laugh at the juice and the stains.

DAD holds out a raspberry to MUM.

DAD Come on. Taste it, love. That's right.

MUM takes a raspberry, eats it.

MUM So sweet.

DAD Delicious and sweet and wild. Come on.

Let yourself go. Let's go wild!

ELAINE Dance, Dad, dance!

They all dance happily; then they stutter to a halt.

They are dejected, exhausted.

DAD exits, leaving MUM and ELAINE alone.

MUM and ELAINE wipe the juice off their faces.

MUM exits.

ELAINE Then he died, and there was nothing more to dance for and nothing more to sing for.

Let me out!

No answer.

ELAINE is back in the present, alone, in her bedroom. She puts away her writing things.

ELAINE Chuck this mess away. This is me.

My name is Elaine. Elaine Grew.
This is the story of my Wild Boy.
And he's gone, but it's true.

She digs down into her canvas bag. She lifts some pictures from the table.

ELAINE Look, there's things to show it really happened. Here's the lock of hair I cut when he was fast asleep. Here's the pictures he drew to show the things that he can see and we can't see . . . that I can't see. In me head's the weird voice, the way he sang.

She sings weirdly.

ELAINE On me hands is the weird touch of him. In me memory is the weird weird story of him. Keep watching. Keep looking. Keep listening. It starts way back, months back, in a time of doom and gloom and tribulation. Me dad was six months dead. Me lovely dad.

She sings, and shakes the seedhead.

ELAINE It never woke him.

She shakes the seedhead.

ELAINE Look. This is what it was like.

She shakes the seedhead and dances, and she is carried again into the past.

This time she is in her bedroom, soon after her dad has died.

SCENE ONE

MUM Elaine! Elaine!

Mum enters. Elaine rattles her seedhead, sings and dances wildly.

MUM Elaine! How many times do I have to tell you?

They struggle over the seedhead.

MUM You're driving me insane, lass!

ELAINE Leave me alone! Gerroff me!

Elaine retreats to a corner.

MUM Look at us. We were so happy.

ELAINE I was never happy!

MUM And you were such a lovely girl.

ELAINE I was never lovely. I've always been stupid stupid stupid.

MUM The school's been on the phone again. You've got to go in every day, Elaine, or we'll be in court before we know it, and what'll that lead to?

ELAINE School! School! Full of dooleys and dipsticks just like me.

MUM Don't say dooley. You're my lovely girl, Elaine.

ELAINE rattles the seedhead, dances and sings.

ELAINE Rattle rattle! Dooley dipstick thicko dense. Can't read, can't write, can't see straight, can't think straight, can't—

MUM Oh, Elaine!

ELAINE Can't . . . anything. Rattle rattle. Can't even wake the dead!

MUM STOP . . . THAT . . . NOISE!

MUM exits.

ELAINE shakes the seedhead more slowly.

We move back into the bedroom in the present.

ELAINE Aye, we started to fight like that. Fight like cat and dog and cry like babies and run off from each other and hide in corners from each other . . . So awful.

ELAINE takes a drawing from the table.

ELAINE I'm good at drawing. This is a picture I did of me dad. Ages back. I did it in his allotment. Laid the paper on a cold frame and drew him as he worked. There he is, leaning over the earth and the sun shining down and the sky so blue and the larkybirds singing singing high above.

She softly shakes the seedhead. It carries her back into the past, to the allotment.

DAD enters, whistling softly.

ELAINE leans over her picture, as if drawing it again.

DAD crouches, picks a broken eggshell from the earth.

DAD Come and see.

ELAINE What?

DAD Come and see, love.

ELAINE goes to him.

ELAINE What is it?

DAD A lark's egg. See? Speckled white outside. And brilliant white inside. A chick came out from this. Can you believe it? A little chick made from a yellow yolk and a salty white that'll one day soon be flying over us and

singing the loveliest of songs.
A miracle. Look! Larks, larks, larks.

They stare into the sky, towards the larks.

ELAINE Can hardly see them, Dad.

DAD That's right. They fly that high they nearly disappear. They fly that high you think they fly right out of the world. But listen. Listen to their wild sweet song. There they are.

They listen, and the larks sing.

DAD That's a lovely picture. How about putting me name on it, eh?

Go on, it'll be OK. I'll help you.

DAD guides her hand as they form the letters together.

DAD D . . . A . . . D. That's right. Dad. Well done. Now put your name as the artist.

E . . . L . . . A . . . I . . . N . . . E. Elaine. See?

There's you and me both written down.

ELAINE Dad. Elaine.

DAD One day soon, we'll have your writing clear as your drawing, eh? Hey. Let's cut some of those massive daisies for your mum. Whoops! Spider.

DAD suddenly plucks something from the air.

DAD You can work spells with these.
Listen:
Spider spider spin your web,
Spider spin around my head.
Spider spider sit dead still,
Spider bring me what I will.
A five-pound note!

DAD flourishes a five-pound note.

DAD It worked!

ELAINE Silly!

DAD crouches, as if tending to his plants.

ELAINE softly rattles. She dreams and wonders as her mind moves between the present and the past.

ELAINE I've got the picture still. Dad. Elaine.

Dad. Elaine. Looks a mess, but I knew what it meant. . . .

The allotment. It was a wild place, a wilderness, and I was his wild girl. The middle of it was all tame and neat, but all around: the long grass, the high weeds, where I crawled and wandered and got lost and called out to him.

DAD Go on, little one.

ELAINE What, Dad?

DAD Go on. Crawl deep into the wilderness. Go on. Get lost in there. Go on. I'll be here. Just call out if you get lost and I'll bring you back to me.

ELAINE crawls and laughs and moves through the wilderness of tall grasses and weeds. She sits up and smiles as she remembers.

ELAINE The allotment. Place of dreams and magic mixed with leeks and spuds and raspberries ever since I was a little little girl. Crawl crawl I went, like a little lizard, crawl crawl like a little snake. Seeds in me eyes and nose, soil on me hands and knees. Crawling crawling further and further into the wild till me dad called—

DAD Elaine! Wild girl! Time to come back out!

ELAINE Yes, Dad!

She shakes the seedhead softly. She dreams and wonders.

ELAINE Rattle rattle. Rattle rattle. Rattle rattle . . . There was often someone else there too. Another man.

McNamara enters, stands peering from his own allotment.

ELAINE McNamara. Had the allotment next to Dad's. Beady eyes, beady stare. Always watching us, he was, always sneering at us. His place was all neat and trim with peas and beans and onions in neat trim rows.

McNAMARA Look at it. Look at the state of it. Like a damn jungle. Hey! What if we all let our gardens go like that, eh?

DAD Eh?

McNAMARA I said, what if we all let our gardens go like that? Get it tidied up, man.

DAD It's tidy enough for us.

McNAMARA	Eh? And what about the effect you're having on that poor lass?
DAD	There's nothing wrong with her.
McNAMARA	Nothing wrong! She'll turn out daft as you are. Poor girl.
ELAINE	Usually he said nothing, just watched, just stared. Leaned on his fence and sneered and stared and shook his head and clicked his tongue and stared and stared and stared.

McNamara shakes his head and clicks his tongue and exits.

DAD	I ever show you how to grow a fairy, pet?
ELAINE	A fairy, Daddy?
DAD	A fairy.
ELAINE	There's no such thing as fairies!
DAD	Yes, there is. But nobody knows you got to grow them first, like they was leeks or raspberries. A bit of horse muck'll help, and a bit of spit.

DAD plucks a fairy seed from the air. He holds it on his palm.

DAD — Look! Here's a fairy seed. Spit on it.

They spit together on the fairy seed.

DAD — Whisper a spell:

Come along, my little fairy, grow
like mushroom, grow like magic,
grow like happiness in the heart . . .

ELAINE — Silly!

DAD — Put it gently on the ground.

DAD puts the fairy seed on the earth, puts horse muck and water on it.

DAD — Then the horse muck. Then the water.
Then spit again.

They spit again.

DAD — Then just wait.

ELAINE — How long?

DAD — That's the mystery. You can never tell. Some fairies take ninety-nine years to grow . . .

ELAINE	Ninety-nine years!
DAD	And some just take ninety-nine minutes. Or ninety-nine days. Or ninety-nine blinks of an eye. Go on, blink ninety-nine times, keep on wishing and see if the fairy grows.

They blink and count quickly together and end up in laughter.

DAD	Not enough. No fairy. Ah, well. Mebbe this one's a ninety-nine yearer.
ELAINE	Silly!

DAD exits.

ELAINE softly shakes the seedhead.

She wonders and dreams, and moves between the present and the past.

ELAINE	We had fairies planted everywhere in Dad's allotment. All we ever got of course was spuds and leeks and raspberries. Except each night when the fairies jumped out of the earth and danced like wind and fire in me dreams. I used to draw them, draw me dreams. Fairies!

McNamara enters.

Elaine is drawn back into the past, into the allotment. He watches her, shakes his head, clicks his tongue.

McNAMARA Fairies! Ha! Ha! He's leading you astray, little lady. He doesn't want you to grow up. He's turning you into a little stupid wild thing.

ELAINE No, he's not! No, he's not!

McNamara exits.

ELAINE Was it silly? Was it baby stuff? That's what Mum said. That's what they all said. Their voices were all around me. Their voices echoed through my head.

Elaine holds her hands around her head as the voices start.

SCENE TWO

THE CHORUS OF VOICES

(They are the voices of neighbors, classmates and teachers.)

—Have you seen the way she just stares out the window with her gob hanging open?

—Like she's catching flies.

—Like a little kid.

—Like a baby.

—And the state of her books?

—Like a spider's crawled over them.

—Like somebody's chucked spaghetti on them.

—Hey, Elaine, has somebody chucked spaghetti on your book?

—No, that's her writing, man!

—Now, leave Elaine alone. Oh dear, Elaine. We're going to have to do better than that, aren't we?

—Concentrate, girl!

—Keep your mind on your work.

—Elaine has severe difficulty in maintaining concentration on the task in hand.

—Reading: accuracy?

—Nil.

—Comprehension?

—Nil.

—Reading age?

—Elaine has not yet achieved a score in our current methods of assessment.

—Writing skills?

—Hahahahahahaha!

—She's just out of it, man.

—Round the bend.

—Up the pole.

—Doolally.

—She's upset, man. She's in grief.

—Why's that, then?

—Her dad . . .

—He was a one, eh?

—Aye, I know, but he died, didn't he?

—Aye.

—Poor soul, eh?

—Aye, poor soul.

—Aye.

—Hey. Listen: Dad's dead and she's losing her head.

—Dad's dead and you're losing your head,

—Dad's dead and you're losing your head,

—Dad's dead and you're—

ELAINE Stop it! Stop it! Stop it!

MUM comes in, hurries to comfort ELAINE.

MUM Oh, Elaine, take no notice of them, love.

Mum holds Elaine tight, then holds her at arm's length.

MUM But Elaine—you just got to start getting on with it.

ELAINE I don't know how. I don't know how!

Elaine and Mum exit.

SCENE THREE

In the house, MUM is alone. There's a knock on the door. McNAMARA enters, carrying a tray of beautifully presented vegetables, fruits and flowers.

MUM	Oh, Mr. McNamara.
McNAMARA	I hope I'm not disturbing you.
MUM	Not at all. Please come in.
McNAMARA	I brought you some veg from the allotment . . .
MUM	For us?
McNAMARA	. . . and some flowers from my garden.
MUM	Oh, you shouldn't have.
McNAMARA	I thought I should tell you . . . I saw Elaine up at the allotment this morning.

ELAINE enters. She recoils when she sees McNAMARA.

ELAINE	What you doing here? What's he doing here?

MUM	Calm down, love. It's only Mr. McNamara. He's brought some veg for us. Look. Look at this beautiful tomato.
ELAINE	It's poison!
MUM	Oh, Elaine.
ELAINE	He's spit on it. He's put a spell on it. It's poison. Don't touch it! I wouldn't eat it if I was dying of hunger! It's puke! Yuck! You should see his allotment. It's a disgrace! What's he doing here?
MUM	Elaine, Mr. McNamara says he's seen you out and about when you should be at school. He's seen you in your dad's allotment.
ELAINE	Spy! Spy! He's always staring, watching with his evil eye. He thought Dad was stupid and messy and . . . and he thinks I am as well. Always did, right from when I was a little girl.
MUM	Take no notice, Mr. McNamara.
ELAINE	Mum!
MUM	It's because he's worried about you. Because he cares for us!

McNAMARA	I've always been concerned about you, Elaine.
ELAINE	Mum! Can you not see?
MUM	I'm sorry, Mr. McNamara.
ELAINE	I'm not! I'm not!
McNAMARA	I understand. It's so difficult. A spirit like hers, and no man in the house . . .
ELAINE	What? Mum?
MUM	Why don't you leave us, Mr. McNamara? I'll calm her down.

McNamara exits. Mum turns angrily to Elaine.

MUM	Now then, madam . . .

SCENE FOUR

ELAINE is in the allotment. She keeps reaching to the earth, pushing undergrowth aside, searching.

ELAINE — No fairy. No fairy. No fairy. No fairy.
Daddy! Daddy! Daddy!

She catches a seed in midair. She spits at it.

ELAINE — Grow like mushroom, grow like magic, grow like happiness in the heart.

She spits at it again, plants it in the earth, puts horse muck on it.
She blinks her eyes fast.

ELAINE — Grow like mushroom. Grow like magic.
Grow like happiness in the heart.
One two three four five six seven eight . . .
Daddy!

MCNAMARA enters, watches from his own allotment.

ELAINE looks around, sees him. She catches a spider.

ELAINE — Spider! Big fat spider.
You can make spells with spiders.
Spider spider spin your web,

Spider spin around my head.
Spider spider sit dead still,
Spider work my wicked will.
Kill McNamara! Ah!

ELAINE puts the spider down. She turns to MCNAMARA again.

He continues to watch in silence.

ELAINE spits in despair. She sits on the earth. She takes out paper and pencil from her canvas bag, begins to draw. She takes out her seedhead. She sings and rattles to herself, rocks back and forward.

The WILD BOY comes out from the wilderness. He watches her. He weirdly joins in with her song.

ELAINE Oh!

WILD BOY reaches out towards ELAINE.

ELAINE Don't you dare! Who are you?

They circle each other. Larks sing high above. The WILD BOY indicates them with his hands—a gesture of great tenderness.

ELAINE Skylarks. Yes, they're beautiful.

WILD BOY sings weirdly again—a discordant imitation of lark song.

ELAINE Who are you? Are you wagging it as well? Which school are you at?

Wild Boy discordantly imitates Elaine's voice.

ELAINE You can't talk! That's all right.
I can't write.
They call me stupid for it, but I'm not.
I'm not!

She reaches out, touches his hands.

ELAINE Fur. What are you?
I can draw, though. Look. I'll draw you.

She draws Wild Boy.

ELAINE Look. This is you. This is . . .
What's your name?
I'll call you . . . Wild Boy.
I can't write it.

She makes a few scribbles to indicate his name.

ELAINE There. Best I can do. Ha. And here's my name. Elaine. I can just do that.
That's who I am. Say my name, Elaine.
E-laine.

Wild Boy weirdly imitates her.

Suddenly, Elaine remembers McNamara.

ELAINE Quick! Get back in the weeds where he can't see you.

Wild Boy doesn't go back.

McNamara shakes his head, sighs.

McNAMARA Silly girl. Stop talking to thin air.
Pull yourself together. Get out of there.
Get back to school before your mother loses her wits.

He continues to shake his head and sigh as he watches.

ELAINE He hasn't seen you. Say my name.
E-laine.

WILD BOY E-ay.

ELAINE Elaine.

WILD BOY E-ay.

ELAINE That's right! That's nearly right!
Oh, Wild Boy! Draw me.
Go on. It's your turn. You draw me.

She pushes the pencil and paper into his hands.

He inspects them, confused.

ELAINE Just draw what you see.

He moves the pencil across the paper.

ELAINE Is this what you see? Is this really what you see? Oh, Wild Boy! Are you a fairy? Did you grow from the fairy seed I planted with me dad ninety-nine weeks ago?

ELAINE gently touches him, inspects him.

ELAINE No wings. Heavy. Fur on your hands and feet. You're . . . ugly. No, not ugly. Come with me. Come on. Come on.

ELAINE tugs his hand. He holds back, glances towards MCNAMARA.

ELAINE Just take no notice of him. He doesn't see you, does he? He doesn't see! Come on, quick! Come with me. Oh, come on, Wild Boy. Let's go home!

They leave the allotment together. The lark song intensifies.

Wild Boy gazes up to the larks, gestures towards them again, imitates their song.

Elaine laughs joyfully and tugs at him, and they hurry away.

SCENE FIVE

THE CHORUS OF VOICES

The voices commentate on E*LAINE's return home from the allotment.*

—Did you see?

—Eh?

—That lass. That Elaine.

—Her again.

—Aye. Did you see her coming down from the allotments?

—Talking to thin air.

—Laughing at thin air.

—Singing at thin air.

—Babbling and laughing like a daft thing, she was.

—Babbling and laughing and pointing at the larks in the sky.

—Too much sun, mebbe.

—It has been blazing hot.

—They put you away for that, you know.

—They don't.

—They do.

—Put you away and chuck away the key.

—They'll come and get her, eh?

—Aye. A big white van and big strong nurses.

—Come on, Elaine, they'll say.

—Come on, love, we'll not harm you.

—This won't hurt a bit.

—Poor soul.

—Aye, poor soul.

—Hee hee hee.

—Wouldn't want her playing with my kids.

—Me neither.

—Not safe, letting her run round like that.

—Shouldn't be allowed.

—Lets the estate down.

—Lock her up, that's what I say.

—Aye. Take her away. Lock her up.

—Lock her up!

SCENE SIX

The kitchen. Mum is there.

Elaine and Wild Boy enter.

MUM	Where you been, girl? The school's been on again. You've been wagging it again. What am I going to do with you? Oh, Elaine.
ELAINE	I went to the allotment. I found . . .
MUM	That place again. Why's nobody taken it over yet? Elaine, all it'll do is make you worse.
ELAINE	I found . . .

Elaine gestures towards Wild Boy, showing him to Mum. Mum sees nothing.

MUM	I talked to the school. I talked to the doctors.
ELAINE	The doctors!
MUM	They want to look at you, Elaine. They want to see . . .
ELAINE	See what?

MUM See what's wrong. See if there's anything they can do. . . .

ELAINE holds WILD BOY in front of her mum.

WILD BOY smiles tenderly into MUM's eyes.

ELAINE realizes that MUM sees nothing.

ELAINE Look, Mum. Look. Oh, Wild Boy, she can't see you. She can't see!

MUM moves close to ELAINE, peers into her eyes.

MUM Elaine, what's going on in there? What's happened to my little girl?

SCENE SEVEN

ELAINE's bedroom. Night. The moon shines in through the window.

ELAINE is at the table. WILD BOY sits on the table.

ELAINE	Larks soar against the sun by day, bats flicker-flack against the moon by night. You see them, Wild Boy? Flicker-flack, wild wings in the night.
	Say my name. Elaine. E-laine.
WILD BOY	E-ay.

ELAINE shows him a drawing of the moon, then points at the window and the moon.

ELAINE	That's the moon, Wild Boy. That's the moon that lights the night and pulls the seas and drives us wild. Moooon.
WILD BOY	Oooooo!

ELAINE shakes the seedhead. She starts to dance and yell and sing.

She draws WILD BOY into the dance. He weirdly sings and yells along with her.

ELAINE Dance, my wild boy. Dance!

MUM (*from outside the room*)

Elaine! Elaine!

They continue to dance and yell. MUM *enters.*

MUM What's going on in here?

ELAINE Just dancing, Mum.

MUM You'll bring the house down. You'll . . .

ELAINE I'll what?

MUM You'll drive me wild.

MUM *looks around the room. She does not see* WILD BOY, *but she appears to feel that something is wrong.*

WILD BOY *moves close to her, peers closely at her.*

ELAINE What do you see, Mum?

MUM What do you mean? Nothing. Your room. What's that . . . ?

ELAINE That what?

MUM That . . . smell or something. No, not a smell.

Mum moves closer to Wild Boy. She sniffs, narrows her eyes.

ELAINE	Look closer, Mum. Closer.
MUM	What did you do today, at the allotment?
ELAINE	Just mooched. Just dreamed. Just remembered.
MUM	No fairies?
ELAINE	No fairies.
MUM	I love you. You know that, don't you?
ELAINE	Yes.
MUM	You're such a brave girl.
ELAINE	No, I'm not.
MUM	When the doctors look at you . . .
ELAINE	They'll see nothing.
MUM	It's because they want to see what they can do for you.
ELAINE	They'll do nothing.

MUM It's because I love you, love.

ELAINE I know that. Look closely, Mum. Please.

Look with your . . . inside eye.

MUM Inside eye. Oh, Elaine, what nonsense is that?

I'm looking closely at my lovely girl.

ELAINE Look closer. See what you can see.

Mum kisses her cheek, hugs her.

MUM Oh, Elaine. It's so hard for you. Even harder than it is for me. But things'll get better, my little love. Sleep tight. Sweet dreams.

Mum exits.

ELAINE She doesn't see. She doesn't see you, Wild Boy. . . .

SCENE EIGHT

A doctor's surgery. On the wall are diagrams of the eye and the brain, and an eye-test chart.

The DOCTOR *and* ELAINE *face each other.*

MUM *watches nervously.*

WILD BOY *stands apart, watching, then begins to move through the room, inspecting it.*

DOCTOR	Look at the letters, Elaine. Tell me which ones you can see.
ELAINE	One that's like a tree and one that's like a tent and a moon and a half a moon and they slither and slide. . . .
MUM	She can't read, Doctor. Not a single word.
DOCTOR	We all have our cross to—
ELAINE	It's not a cross.
DOCTOR	I'd like you to look at these now.

The DOCTOR *shows* ELAINE *a series of cards containing blots and blotches.*

DOCTOR	Just say what you see, Elaine. Don't

worry. Nobody's trying to catch you out. Just say what you see. Come on, try to take part.

MUM — D'you realize what this is costing, Elaine?

ELAINE — I see a larkybird's heart thumping in the dark. I see the onions run to seed. I see me mum's tongue flapping and flipping when she whispers I was such a lovely girl. I see me dad . . .

DOCTOR — What?

MUM — Your dad what?

ELAINE — I see him planting fairies in the garden.

DOCTOR — Fairies?

MUM — She's turning back into a baby, Doctor. Her dad was lovely, but some of the things he told her . . .

ELAINE — Fairies. He's got spit and horse muck on his hands. We count to ninety-nine . . .

Wild Boy! We grew a wild boy, not a fairy!

DOCTOR A wild boy?

ELAINE A wild boy!

She looks at WILD BOY and laughs.

DOCTOR What are you looking at now, Elaine?

What are you seeing now?

The DOCTOR goes to ELAINE with an eye torch in his hand. She recoils but he holds her. He shines it into her eye.

DOCTOR Just stay calm, Elaine. I need to look inside, deep inside.

ELAINE What you looking at? Get off! Get off!

WILD BOY moves to the DOCTOR'S back. He pulls the DOCTOR'S hand away from ELAINE.

The DOCTOR is alarmed, amazed, uncomprehending.

ELAINE goes to WILD BOY. They hold hands and laugh. They begin to dance and sing.

The DOCTOR pulls himself together, takes a notebook from his pocket, begins to write as he watches ELAINE'S antics.

She giggles at him, then plucks a spider from the air before her face.

ELAINE Spider!

Spider spider spin your web,

Spider spin into my head.

Spider spider sit dead still,

Spider work my wicked will.

Doctor, be gone!

She giggles, seeing that nothing happens to the DOCTOR.

ELAINE Ah, well, it doesn't always work. Pretty spider.

She runs to the eye-test chart, points to the letters.

ELAINE That's E for Elaine. That's D for Dad.

That's M for Mum.

That's W for Wild Boy. See!

Dance, Wild Boy, dance!

ELAINE *dances, yells and sings with* WILD BOY.

The DOCTOR *gives up writing, goes to* MUM.

MUM Stop it, Elaine! You'll . . .

ELAINE I know I will. Dance, Wild Boy, dance!

Dance and yell.

Yell that hard we'll wake the dead!

ELAINE and WILD BOY run off, leaving the DOCTOR and MUM disturbed and bemused.

SCENE NINE

Elaine's bedroom. Night. The moon shines through the window.

Wild Boy is on the bed, staring at the moon.

Elaine crouches with her ear to the floor; listening.

ELAINE	McNamara. He's been here for hours downstairs with Mum.
WILD BOY	Oooooo.
ELAINE	That's right. Moon. Mooooon.
WILD BOY	Moooon.
ELAINE	Yes! E-laine.
WILD BOY	E-laine.
ELAINE	Yes! Yes! You can talk! What's your name?
WILD BOY	E-laine.
ELAINE	No. That's my name.
WILD BOY	E-laine?
ELAINE	No. Your name. Never mind. Where

did you come from? You understand? Where did you come from? Draw it!

WILD BOY draws. He now has more control over the pencil. He passes what he has drawn to ELAINE.

ELAINE That's me, isn't it? But draw me other things.

WILD BOY draws again. As he draws, he looks around him, as if seeing things that ELAINE cannot see.

ELAINE What are these, Wild Boy? Where do you see these?

WILD BOY points into the spaces around them.

He tries to show her what he sees.

ELAINE Here? Now? I see nothing.

WILD BOY laughs and murmurs, as if communicating with another.

He puts down the paper and pencils and begins to dance, as if with another.

ELAINE watches in fascination and frustration.

ELAINE Who you dancing with, Wild Boy? Oh, if I could see through your eyes.

SCENE NINE

McNAMARA (*from outside*)

Elaine! Elaine Grew!

ELAINE McNamara!

McNamara comes in, switches the light on.

ELAINE MUM!

McNAMARA Your mum will see you later. She told me about your performance today in the doctor's.

He picks up the scattered drawings. He paces the room, looking about him.

Wild Boy follows him closely, watches him closely.

McNAMARA You have to learn the ways of the world, girl.

ELAINE What are you doing here?

McNAMARA You have to knuckle down. You have to control yourself.

ELAINE You're nothing to do with me!

McNAMARA These things, for instance. They're like products of a twisted mind.

ELAINE Spider spider spin your web, Spider spin around my head. . . .

Wild Boy moves closer to McNamara, holds his face close to his.

McNAMARA What's that . . . smell or something?

ELAINE Spider spider sit dead still,

Spider work my wicked will. . . .

McNAMARA I saw you, as a little girl, wriggling through the grass, crawling through the weed, slithering through the mud.

I heard him, urging you on.

ELAINE Kill McNamara!

McNAMARA She'll grow up wrong, I used to say. You got to train kids proper, just like plants. You got to stake them and prune them and shape them. Otherwise . . . She's growing up wrong, I used to say. And after all these years, you've growed up wrong, Elaine Grew. Growed up wrong, like a plant gone wild. You need training. . . .

He crumples the drawings, breaks pencils, takes up the seedhead and discards it again.

WILD BOY's stance becomes more sinister, more threatening.

McNAMARA Put away the things of childhood,

Elaine Grew.

ELAINE Kill McNamara. Kill!

McNAMARA Crawl back out of the wilderness.

ELAINE Kill McNamara! Kill!

McNAMARA Come into the real world. What's that . . . smell or something?

ELAINE Spider spider spin your web . . .

WILD BOY's face is almost touching McNAMARA's.

McNAMARA What's that . . . something. Agh, something!

ELAINE Spider spin around my head . . .

McNAMARA What d'you get up to here, in the darkness, on your own?

ELAINE Spider spider sit dead still . . .

McNAMARA One day, maybe soon . . .

ELAINE Spider work my wicked will.

MCNAMARA . . . I will take your father's part.

ELAINE Kill McNamara. Kill!

MCNAMARA One day, maybe very soon.

ELAINE Shut him up!

WILD BOY clamps his hand across MCNAMARA's mouth.

MCNAMARA recoils in shock, then retreats slowly.

WILD BOY follows, as if herding MCNAMARA out.

MCNAMARA What do you get up to in here, in the dark, in the light of the moon? What's that . . . something? Wild girl. Wild girl. We'll have to tame you.

MCNAMARA exits.

WILD BOY dances in triumph.

ELAINE burns with anger.

ELAINE Mooooooon!

WILD BOY Oooooooooo!

SCENE TEN

ELAINE's bedroom. Later the same night.

ELAINE and WILD BOY crouch on her bed, bathed in moonlight.

ELAINE has been cutting paper into the shapes of letters.

She holds up letters in random patterns.

WILD BOY watches, as if determined to listen and learn.

ELAINE — I've made a word out of letters. It's a name, your name. Don't know what it says, but when I say it I say Skoosh.

Skoosh!

Lovely sound, lovely word, lovely name. Where do sounds and words and names come from? From deep in the deep in the deep of your heart.

Where do letters come from? From a tabletop, from the point of a pen, from the pictures running round the walls. How do you make the noises from inside your heart match up with letters in the world?

I don't know. I'll call you Skoosh.

She holds the letters before her mouth as she speaks the word.

She throws the letters into the air and lets them scatter.

Wild Boy laughs and plays at catching the letters.

ELAINE How does it happen? How do you make the letters catch the word? How do you make the sound catch the letters? I can't do it, but I make the sound. Skoosh. The letters don't matter. Skoosh! Skoosh!

Mum enters. She stand in the doorway, watching.

ELAINE What is your name?

WILD BOY Skoosh.

ELAINE What is my name?

WILD BOY Elaine.

ELAINE See? Hear? I taught him how to talk.

MUM I'm keeping you in, my girl!

ELAINE Mum!

MUM I'm at the end of my tether. What can I do? I'm locking you in.

Mum exits, closing the door.

Elaine rushes to the door, finds it locked.

She rattles the window.

ELAINE Door locked. Window locked. Let me out!

No way out, my Wild Boy Skoosh.

WILD BOY Skoosh.

ELAINE Hahaha. Skoosh!

WILD BOY Mooooon!

ELAINE Moooooooon!

Skoosh! Listen. We'll make a wilderness here in my room. We'll make a garden where we can crawl like lizards, like snakes, where we can slither deep into the wild.

WILD BOY Wiiiiild!

ELAINE Yes, Wild Boy. Now, what do we need?

Soil, plants, sunlight, rain. Useless.

Elaine runs to the door and the window, rattles them.

ELAINE Let me out!

WILD BOY (*trying to imitate Elaine*)

E eee ou! E ee ou!

ELAINE Shh. No. Listen, Wild Boy Skoosh.

My dad . . . Yes, my dad. You don't know my dad but he was wonderful. My dad said that the greatest of all gardens is the mind. He said in the mind you can grow anything. Anything!

WILD BOY E-y-ing.

ELAINE Anything, that's right. We can dream a garden. We can imagine a garden. Dream it, Wild Boy. Close your eyes and watch it grow.

Elaine closes her eyes, dreams and imagines.

Wild Boy copies her, keeps glancing at her to check that he's imagining properly.

ELAINE You have to see the onions and raspberries and leeks and the flowers, and you have to feel the soil in your fingers and under your feet and you have to feel where the edge of the wilderness is . . .

WILD BOY I-er-ess.

ELAINE That's right. Wilderness! Can you see it and feel it, Wild Boy Skoosh? Can you smell the soil and the scents of the flowers and feel the sun on you and the breeze and . . . Can you see anything, Skoosh?

WILD BOY is becoming distracted. He looks away from ELAINE, towards the moonlight pouring through the window, towards the outside world.

ELAINE opens her eyes, calls to him. But he has grown lethargic.

ELAINE Skoosh!

WILD BOY (*halfheartedly*)

Skoosh!

ELAINE Look, this is the earth and these are raspberries and this is a chrysanthemum and this is the edge of the . . . Let me out!

WILD BOY E ee ou!

ELAINE Mum!

WILD BOY U!

ELAINE Let me out!

MUM (*from outside*)

Elaine! Elaine, just calm down, love!

ELAINE Let me out!

MUM (*from outside*)

Oh, Elaine. Be a good girl, will you?

ELAINE Let me out! Let me out!

WILD BOY clambers onto the bed. He lies there, dispirited.

ELAINE becomes more desperate, more yearning.

ELAINE Oh, isn't it lovely here, Skoosh? The sun, the air. Can you hear those lovely lovely larkybirds? Look, Wild Boy Skoosh. This is the edge of the wilderness—the long grass, the high weeds. I'll crawl in there, like a little lizard, like a little snake.

ELAINE crawls, as if she's in the wilderness of the allotment, shouldering aside weeds and grasses. There is lark song.

ELAINE Crawl crawl. Seeds in me eyes and nose, soil on me hands and knees.

Oh, look: here's a lark come down!

SCENE TEN

The song of the lark brings a change.

The bedroom and the allotment merge once more.

Wild Boy exits. Dad enters, whistling softly.

DAD Go on, little one. Crawl deep into the wilderness. Go on. Get lost in there. Go on. I'll be here. Just call out if you get lost and I'll bring you back to me.

ELAINE Daddy!

Elaine doesn't look back.

DAD Elaine! Elaine! Wild girl! Time to come back out.

MUM (*from outside*)

Elaine! Elaine!

Dad exits. Mum comes into the room.

MUM Elaine! Elaine! What you doing? Elaine?

What you doing on the floor?

Who you been talking to?

ELAINE Mum. Is he still there?

Elaine doesn't look back.

MUM Who? Who?

ELAINE Oh, Mum, look closely.

MUM Oh, Elaine, there's nothing. There's nobody.

ELAINE Can you at least see the long grass and the raspberries and hear the larkybirds singing singing . . . ?

MUM Oh, my little love.

Elaine turns and looks.

ELAINE There's nobody. There's not even Skoosh now.

MUM Oh, Elaine.

Elaine crouches on the floor, stares into the empty room.

ELAINE Skoosh! Skoooooosh!

SCENE ELEVEN

THE CHORUS OF VOICES

—She's crackers, of course.

—Really crackers. Right round the twist.

—Have you heard her? Howling and yowling.

—Chanting and ranting.

—Making a noise fit to wake the dead.

—If you're lucky you'll see her.

—See her?

—Aye. Just watch the window.

—See her dancing like a loony.

—See her banging on the windows.

—Hear her yelling, Let me out!

—Let me out!

—Let me out!

—Her mum must be at the end of her tether, eh?

—Aye. Poor soul.

—Poor soul.

—Thank God she's locked her in.

—Aye. And let's hope she's chucked the key away.

—Don't want something like that running round the place.

—Little wild thing howling and yowling.

—Little monster chanting and ranting.

—Little devil doing . . .

—Just imagine what she could do.

—Such awful things.

—Here! We got kids of our own out here, you know!

—Keep that wild thing under lock and key!

—We got kids to keep safe out here!

—Just imagine if she got hold of a child of yours.

—Aye.

—Aye . . .

—Just imagine if *she* was a child of yours.

—No.

—No . . .

—Don't bear thinking of.

SCENE TWELVE

The doctor's surgery. ELAINE *is dejected, exhausted. She sits opposite the* DOCTOR.

MUM *stands nervously watching.*

DOCTOR — And what did this wild boy look like, Elaine?

MUM — Come on, love. Please join in.

ELAINE — This tall. Arms and legs, just like us.

A head, just like us. He was just like us.

ELAINE *looks around the room, as if seeking* WILD BOY.

ELAINE — I keep thinking he'll come back. But I think he went back to the allotment.

DOCTOR — And what else, Elaine? Did he have wings or anything like that?

ELAINE — Wings? Don't be daft.

DOCTOR — A tail, maybe?

ELAINE — Are you joking?

DOCTOR	OK. So what was it that made him . . . wild?
ELAINE	He came out of the wilderness . . .
DOCTOR	The wilderness?
MUM	Her dad's allotment, Doctor. It was always such a mess.
ELAINE	It wasn't a mess. It was beautiful!
	He couldn't talk . . .
	I taught him how to talk. So I can't be that stupid, can I?
MUM	Of course you're not stupid, love.
ELAINE	And he could sing like the larks. And there was fur on his hands and feet.
DOCTOR	Fur, Elaine?
ELAINE	Fur. Yes, fur.
DOCTOR	Ah. And . . . the kind of fur? Like a cat, maybe, or a bear, or . . .
	What else has fur? Like a fluffy toy, perhaps.

ELAINE — See, you don't believe me. Nobody'll ever believe me.

MUM — But, love, you've got to see, it's so . . .

ELAINE — Dad would have. Dad would have believed.

Dad would have seen him as well!

Wild Boy! Skoosh! Where are you?

SCENE THIRTEEN

Elaine's bedroom. Daytime. ELAINE *is crawling on the floor, as if in the allotment.*

MUM *and* MCNAMARA *stand watching.*

ELAINE *is absorbed in her own actions and doesn't see them there.*

ELAINE — I'll grow him again. That's what I'll do.

I'll grow him again.

She catches a fairy seed, spits on it, plants it.

ELAINE — Fairy seed. Horse muck. Spit. In the ground. One two three four five six seven . . .

No fairy. No Wild Boy.

She crawls again.

ELAINE — Crawl deeper, Elaine. Crawl like a lizard, crawl like a snake.

MUM — They said it's grief. They said it's just her age. They said to keep an eye on her. They said she might just start getting better. But they said if she doesn't . . .

McNAMARA What can I do? Elaine. Elaine!

McNamara moves towards Elaine, but Mum holds him back. Elaine plucks a spider from the earth.

ELAINE Spider spider spin your web.

MUM She gets so lost in her own world.

ELAINE Spider spin around my head.

MUM Can't hear, can't see.

ELAINE Spider spider sit dead still.

McNAMARA Elaine. Elaine!

ELAINE Spider bring me what I will. Wild Boy. Wild Boy!

MUM Elaine. Elaine! Where are you?

ELAINE Horse muck. Spit. Grow like mushroom, grow like magic.

One two three four five . . .

MUM Elaine! Elaine!

Elaine looks up, sees Mum there.

ELAINE Mum! Fancy seeing you here. Isn't it lovely? Come on in.

MUM What, love?

ELAINE Come on in.

MUM Oh, Elaine!

MUM looks at MCNAMARA. She wants to join in with her daughter, but the man's presence inhibits her, embarrasses her.

ELAINE Come on, Mum. Please join in.

Crawl like a lizard, crawl like a snake.

Crawl deep into the wilderness.

MUM Oh, Elaine.

ELAINE Oh, Mum. It's what Dad would have said.

MUM sighs, glances at MCNAMARA, then joins ELAINE in the imaginary allotment.

She crawls beside ELAINE.

MUM Where are we, love?

ELAINE We're at the allotment, Mum. Look, the grass, the weeds, the sun shining down, the larkybirds singing.

Mum looks around the room.

MUM We're in your bedroom, love.

ELAINE Can you not see, can you not hear, can you not smell?

MUM Yes, love.

ELAINE Good. We might find a fairy in here, you know.

MUM A fairy?

ELAINE Yes, a real fairy. You can grow them, you know.

MUM Really? Oh, love. Give me a cuddle, love.

Mum and Elaine hug each other.

ELAINE You don't believe me, do you?

MUM I do.

ELAINE You can't see anything, can you?

MUM Yes, I can.

ELAINE Come with me to the allotment.

MUM Oh, Elaine.

ELAINE You've never been, have you, not since . . . You used to come. Do you remember?

Do you remember how we used to dance there, all of us together?

ELAINE tugs her mum's hand. She yearns to leave the house and take her mother with her, but MUM holds back, undecided.

McNAMARA You'll mess her up even worse. You'll mess yourself up.

MUM looks at him, listens to him, holds ELAINE.

McNAMARA Give her rules and regulations.

Discipline her. Tame her.

It's like gardening. How d'you get the best plants?

Proper feeding, proper watering, proper pruning. Start growing the wrong way and you pull them back.

Start getting wild and you cut them back. You show them what's the right way and what's the wrong way to grow. You train them, and you keep on training them, otherwise there's just . . . wilderness.

ELAINE Come with me, Mum.

MUM smiles, turns away from MCNAMARA and hurries off with ELAINE.

MCNAMARA shakes his head, sighs, slowly follows.

SCENE FOURTEEN

THE CHORUS OF VOICES

They comment on the journey out of the estate.

—Did you see them?

—Who?

—Daft Elaine Grew and her mother, man.

—The crazy one?

—Aye. Did you see them walking out the estate? Running up the hill to the allotments?

—Weirdos, eh?

—The kid pulling her mum. That bloke McNamara following them.

—They looked wild, eh?

—Wild. Wild.

—The mother looked as crackers as the kid, eh?

—It happens like that with families.

One of them starts cracking up and before you know it they're all belting round the twist.

—Climbing up the pole.

—Poor souls.

—Aye. Hee hee hee. Poor souls.

—Mebbe they were chasing fairies.

—Or running after things that weren't there.

—Hey, Elaine, bring us a fairy back!

—Did you hear, though?

—Eh?

—Did you hear the birds?

—The birds?

—Aye. Did you hear the way they were singing?

—Now you mention it . . .

—Never heard them that loud.

—And never seen that many.

—Like the sky was filled with larkybirds way up high.

—And the sun that bright and everything that still.

—Weird.

—Aye. Weird.

SCENE FIFTEEN

The allotment. Mum *and* Elaine *enter.*

Mum *looks around her in wonder, touches the earth, the plants, smells the air, feels the sun on her face, listens to the larks that sing high above.*

Her whole body relaxes.

She smiles with Elaine, *and joyful memories move through her.*

Elaine *laughs and draws* Mum *into the weeds and long grasses.* Mum *joins in.*

ELAINE	That's right, Mum. Seeds in your eyes and nose, soil on your hands and knees. Crawl in deeper, deeper. Come on. We might find a fairy in here, you know.
MUM	Might we? A real fairy?
ELAINE	A real fairy.
MUM	Oh, love.
ELAINE	Come on, Mum.
	You can grow them, you know, like they was leeks or raspberries.

Dad showed me. . . . Yes, Dad.

Look, here's a fairy seed!

ELAINE plucks a fairy seed from the air.

ELAINE Spit and horse muck.

She spits on the seed, plants it, throws horse muck onto it.

ELAINE Then the spell:

Come along, my little fairy, grow like mushroom . . .

Come on, Mum. Join in. Say it along with me.

MUM is shy at first, but then joins in more confidently.

MUM/ELAINE (*together*)

Grow like mushroom, grow like magic, grow like happiness in the heart.

ELAINE Come on, Mum.

MUM/ELAINE (*together*)

Grow like mushroom, grow like magic, grow like happiness in the heart.

ELAINE Now spit on it again.

MUM Elaine!

MUM giggles and recoils.

ELAINE Go on. Spit on it.

MUM spits halfheartedly.

ELAINE Properly!

MUM I can't!

ELAINE Yes, you can.

ELAINE demonstrates how to spit properly.

MUM copies her, laughing.

ELAINE Now blink dead fast ninety-nine times.

MUM blinks fast.

MUM Like this?

ELAINE Yes, like this.

They blink and count and laugh together and end in giggles. Then they gaze down at the fairy seed.

ELAINE Ah, well. Mebbe this one's a ninety-nine yearer.

MUM A ninety-nine yearer!

ELAINE Isn't it lovely here, Mum?

MUM Yes. . . .

Remember how we used to dance here?

ELAINE Yes.

MUM Give us a cuddle, love.

The larks sing. MUM and ELAINE hug each other.

WILD BOY emerges from the wilderness. He watches them.

MUM sees him over ELAINE's shoulder.

MUM Oh!

ELAINE Mum?

ELAINE turns and sees WILD BOY.

ELAINE Didn't I tell you? Oh, Wild Boy, I thought you'd gone.

MUM Wild Boy.

WILD BOY I oy.

WILD BOY moves towards them.

MUM reaches out and touches his hands.

MUM Fur! What are you?

ELAINE It's my Wild Boy, Mum.
It's Skoosh.

What's my name?

WILD BOY E-laine.

ELAINE What's your name?

WILD BOY Skoosh!

MUM What's my name?

WILD BOY regards her with great tenderness.

MUM What's my name?

WILD BOY Mum.

ELAINE Oh, Wild Boy!

MUM, ELAINE and WILD BOY begin to dance.

ELAINE Come on, Mum. Come on, Wild Boy.

Let's wake the dead!

They dance and sing, then become still.

ELAINE reaches down into the grass, picks up an eggshell.

ELAINE Here's a lark's egg, Mum.

See, speckled white outside, brilliant white inside. A little lark grew out of this. From yellow yolk and salty white and flew away. A miracle.

MUM A miracle. You were once a yolky little salty thing.

And look at you now, so lovely.

MUM and ELAINE are absorbed by their memories and by the miracle of the eggshell.

WILD BOY exits.

DAD enters, whistling softly. He stands watching his wife and daughter.

Lark song.

ELAINE Oh! Here's a lark come down.

MUM and ELAINE are very still. They do not turn.

DAD Go on. Go on.

Crawl deep into the wilderness.

Just call out if you get lost.

Grow like mushroom, grow like magic, grow like happiness in the heart.

Spider, spider, spin your web.

Wild girls. Wild girls!

Dad watches.

Mum and Elaine remain very still. The larks sing.

ELAINE I love you, Mum.

MUM I love you.

Dad exits.

McNamara enters, carrying raspberries in his hands.

Mum turns.

MUM Mr. McNamara.

McNamara is confused, uncertain.

McNAMARA The larks are so loud today.

MUM Were you watching us?

McNAMARA I tried. I couldn't see. You were in the wilderness.

I saw . . .

MUM What?

ELAINE What?

McNAMARA The larks so loud. The sun so bright . . .

I brought you these.

MUM Raspberries.

McNAMARA They were hanging over my allotment.

I reached deep into the thorns.

ELAINE Dad's.

McNAMARA Yes, your dad's. They're . . . delicious.

Sweeter than any I ever grew.

Mum takes the raspberries from him. She hands one to Elaine.

McNamara exits.

Mum and Elaine eat the raspberries.

MUM Delicious.

ELAINE Raspberries. Delicious and sweet and wild.

They laugh at the juice and the stains.

Wild Boy comes out from the wilderness. He moves around them, but they are so absorbed in each other and in their memories that they do not see him at first. Then they smile together, seeing that he is there. He gestures for them to explore the allotment and its wilderness.

ELAINE Come on, Mum.

Elaine and Mum move into the wilderness.

Wild Boy dances, then follows them.

AFTERWORD

We lived in a small estate on a steep hill in a small Tyneside town. The center was just below us: the square with trees and benches, the Co-op, the Blue Bell, the Jubilee. There was a lovely clutter of buildings and names: Dragone's Cafe; MAYS' FASHION'S; Howes Junk; SPEED THE PLOUGH TAVERN; Le Palais de Dans. Churches and workingmen's clubs, busy streets, long queues at bus stops, a steep high street of pork shops and bakers and fishmongers leading down to our railway station. Then were the warehouses and factories, then much further down was the Tyne, and then Newcastle, packed densely on the opposite bank.

Higher up, above our estate, came emptiness, space and light. I remember bright breezy days, leaving the house, leaving the estate, crossing Rectory Road, walking upwards to the playing fields, then the heather hills at the summit of the town. There was a freedom in walking away from the center, in climbing closer to the massive lark-filled sky.

The allotments were just before the playing fields, squeezed into the space between the houses of Fleming Gardens and Windy Ridge. My grandfather's was the third one up, behind the pointed timber fence. You put your hand through the timbers to unlatch the gate, then stepped onto the cinder path that led past the leek trenches, the chrysanthemums and the cold frames to the greenhouse.

Usually he was waiting there, sitting on a seat of old bricks, gazing out across the fields, puffing on his pipe.

"Aye," he'd say, turning to acknowledge me, wiping his hand across the grin that had flickered on his face. "Aye, aye." And he'd spit, wipe his grin again and turn his face to the fields again.

He was a man of little small talk, with no apparent desire to teach me anything with words. No matter what the season, he wore a dark serge suit, a tightly fastened waistcoat, white shirt, dark tie, checked cloth cap and black Oxford boots.

We shared long easy silences, long hours of doing nothing very much. We pottered in the breathless greenhouse and the breezy garden. We lit smoldering smoky fires of weeds. He held me up as I plunged a watering can into the great rainwater butt and watched the great glug and gush and suck the water made around my hand. We watered leeks and onions. We clipped chrysanthemums and plucked sweet warm tomatoes and wrapped them in *Daily Mirror*s. We swigged from huge bottles of lemonade. He lifted his cap, wiped the sweat from his head, replaced the cap again. He tugged at his tight collar. He puffed on his pipe. He spat from one side of his mouth while holding the pipe clenched in the other. He grinned wryly at me. He said "Aye" and "Aye, aye." He took his watch from his waistcoat pocket and raised his eyes and shook his head at the passing of the day.

If we went back to that time now and leaned on the allotment fence and watched the old man and the boy in there, it might all seem pretty pleasant, pretty aimless, pretty pointless. In some obscure way, though, the boy in there was preparing to be a writer.

Years later I was approached by Sally Goldsworthy, head of education at the Lyric Theatre, Hammersmith. Would I be interested in writing a play to be included in the theater's remarkable program of work for children? I pondered the idea. I sat at my desk before a computer beneath a reading lamp. I contemplated an empty space, a stage, and the memories and sensations of the allotment rushed to fill it.

The smells of turned earth and pipe smoke, onions and leeks and chrysanthemums; the taste of tomatoes and peas and raspberries; the feeling of rough cinders under my feet; the voices of other gardeners, of children yelling far off on the fields. I remembered the factory sirens that wailed at lunchtime, the smell of frying chips from the houses on Windy Ridge. I remembered digging in the dirt with a spoon as an infant, with a spade as a growing boy. I remembered sweat and dirt, blisters on my palms, the sting of sunburn on my neck. I remembered worms and centipedes and beetles, the feeling of them as they moved across an open hand. I remembered the pigeons that wheeled in close, fast flocks over our heads, racing back to the pigeon lofts higher up the hill. Over everything, when I recalled that garden and those days, I heard from high above the endless lovely singing of the larks.

Budding writers often ask for advice. What books must be read? What writing practice must be done? Well, there are libraries full of books to be read and reams of notepaper to be filled, and there are great joys and great benefits to be found in the process. But writing isn't a skill the way, say, tennis is—a skill that can be strengthened and refined by constant rehearsal of particular moves, constant development of particular muscles. If you do nothing but write in preparation for writing you'll become a very dismal writer. Listening to larks while digging with a spoon in the dirt might look like a kid just mucking about, but in the long run it can be as valuable as a couple of hours' extra homework with pen in hand or fingers on the keyboard.

There are other, darker forces at work in *Wild Girl, Wild Boy*, of course. My father died when I was young and when my sisters were much younger. So Elaine's pain is something that I know about. But her story is one of life, not death. She's a bold creative spirit, brave enough to yell and scream at death, brave enough to outface it, brave enough to keep returning to her wilderness and to discover—or create—the means to transcend her pain. This is what the writer does: explores the gardens of the mind, crawls through wilderness, emerges with scratched skin and muddied knees accompanied by words and creatures and images that begin to form themselves into the stories that help to keep the world alive.

Printed stories usually take the form of prose: blocks of print that start at the top left-hand corner of a page, march line by line down to the bottom right, then jump up to the top left again. They're the product of solitary days and weeks and months of scribbling in notebooks, tapping at the keyboard, staring out of the window, hissing in frustration, dreaming, pondering, scribbling again, tapping again, slowly slowly trying to sort a wild tangle of words and notions into a coherent story. In the end, all those lovely lines of print and all those lovely pages look beautifully organized, beautifully controlled.

When I was a boy, and beginning to dream of becoming an author, printed pages were both an inspiration and a hindrance to me. I found them beautiful and I wanted to produce them, but at the same time their beauty intimidated me—they seemed so fixed, so untouchable; the writer who produced them must have such an organized mind. How could I, whose mind seemed a jumble, dare to think that I could do the same?

The fixity of a book and the static beauty of a printed page are illusions. A printed story is just a story caught between covers at a particular time. Caught earlier or later, the story would have a different form. And the untouchable beauty of the page is the work of the typesetter, printer, publisher.

Any good story, no matter how controlled it appears on the page, is not a tame, trapped thing. It still has wildness in it, a yearning to break free of its neat lines and numbered pages. And it does break free. It leaps from the page, and moves far beyond the control of the author, as soon as a reader begins to read it.

Reading is a creative, imaginative act. The reader helps to create the book. Each reader creates a different book. Each reader hears different voices, sees different faces and landscapes. Reading is infected by experiences, expectations, dreams and desires. A story is a living thing that escapes from the page and races and prowls through our imagination.

A play can have even fewer claims to fixity. I began to write *Wild Girl, Wild Boy* as I would a piece of prose—alone in my study in Newcastle. I imagined the empty space, the stage. I began to write Elaine's words. I had a notion of what Elaine looked like, how she sounded, what her room looked like, what her estate looked like, what her mum and dad looked like, how they sounded. . . . They walked and talked and danced in the stagelike space I'd cleared in my mind.

But unlike stories in prose that march line by line from top left to bottom right, all the space filled in by the writer, a story in play form moves down the page in short bursts surrounded by lots of space. Dialogue, names, skimpy stage directions, and that's all. The space around the words is for the director, the actors and the designer to fill.

Pretty soon I was out of my study with a half-finished script and on the train to London to see what would happen to this story when it started to break free.

We workshopped the script in an empty space in Islington: Pop-Up Theatre's director, Mike Dalton; assistant director, Jane Wolfson; four actors; and me. As soon as the lines were spoken, they became something new—at once very like and very unlike the way I'd heard them in my mind. And each time they were respoken, they changed again. I saw what happened in silence in a reader's mind happening in a stagelike space before me.

The story was taking on a new life, was being re-created. It had begun to break away and to prowl through the imaginations of everybody there. Elaine leapt to life, became a real girl in front of me, no longer a notion on a page and in my mind, but a dancing, crawling, singing, yelling character of flesh and blood, born not just from my words but from the skills of an actor.

Rewriting was active and immediate. If a character's words fell flat we tried out other variations of the words.

The half-finished script was soon filled with scribbled notes: my own responses, the responses of the directors and the actors.

We had particular discussions about the character McNamara. In the early draft he was a one-dimensional cardboard cutout: simply sinister, nothing more. I was amazed when an actor showed me how his lines could be spoken to suggest a greater complexity, how there was potential to turn McNamara into a slightly more sympathetic (and believable) character. McNamara remains a sinister force, of course, but I hope I learned to suggest that there might be some true concern and tenderness in him.

I watched and listened and scribbled and discussed and learned. I took my script home, scribbled, pondered, contemplated the stage-space in my mind, reworked, wrote on. I maintained an ongoing e-mail correspondence with Mike Dalton in which we shared our suggestions, our excitements, our doubts. Like a good editor commenting on a story in prose, he was able to pinpoint where a tiny adjustment in particular places would benefit the story overall.

We workshopped again. There were difficulties with pacing, with the sequencing of events. There were clumsy moments. How could we make the chorus of voices work onstage? How could we make the shifts from present to past convincing? I scribbled again, wrote again, the story developed again.

By the time we reached rehearsals, we had the first movements of James Hesford and Mark Pearson's amazingly atmospheric and evocative music. We had the first mock-up of Will Hargreaves' set: a magical thing that could blend Elaine's bedroom with her dad's allotment with a doctor's surgery, that could evoke the movements of Elaine's restless, yearning mind. We also had a cast: Janet Bamford, Mark Huckett, Andrew Oliver, Mandy Vernon-Smith. Here they were, the people who would finally lift the story from my pages and pass it over to an audience. These actors stepped into the story, danced in it, sang in it, laughed and cried in it, made it their own world. The story was re-created yet again.

By now, the script was just about done: only a few adjustments remained, to make the words flow more easily and rhythmically on the tongue and on the air. More and more, I became an observer. Moment by moment, the story moved further away from me.

I left it there, in the rehearsal space in Islington, and went home again to Newcastle to work on other projects. For *Wild Girl, Wild Boy,* as far as I was concerned, all that remained were a couple of e-mails, a couple of phone calls with Mike. While I sat at my desk, the music and the set were completed, the play moved from the space in Islington into a week's rehearsal in its first venue, the Lyric Studio.

I traveled nervously to the first performance. I trembled a little as I went into the theater. An hour before the performance, I opened the door into the dark studio, stepped inside. A last-minute rehearsal was under way. The music played. Beneath the stage lights were the bedroom, the allotment. The moon shone through the window above the bed. Who was that figure who shuffled through the lights, with his wild hair, his ragged clothes, with fur on his hands and feet? Who was that girl, her face transfigured by a weird mixture of despair and delight?

I only paused there for a few astonished seconds, but in those seconds I looked into a world that I'd helped to create, but that no longer needed me. I stepped back through the door, into the everyday light, and waited with the rest of the audience for the first performance to begin.

In the weeks and months that followed, the play traveled across the country. It appeared in theaters, arts centers, school halls. While I got on with my life in Newcastle, Skoosh came out from the wilderness in Manchester, Elaine wept and yelled in Stirling, McNamara announced his theories on child-raising in Aberystwyth, Dad planted fairies in Hemel Hempstead, Mum nibbled raspberries in Brighton. The set was erected, taken down, erected again; the cast traveled hundreds of miles; the music was played and replayed; the stage-spaces were illuminated and then returned to darkness. The audiences came and watched and went home again. The story ran its course and ran its course again until the tour was over.

In the end, of course, none of it exists. There is no Elaine, there is no Wild Boy, there is no allotment, there is no bedroom. The play is a subterfuge, a set of disguises and tricks. It's a pack of lies. The story of Elaine and Skoosh exists in the minds of those who see the story on the stage, and of those who read their story on the page.

Like all stories, it's a pack of lies that tries to reach out to us and allow us to experience some kind of human truth. Of course it depends on the creative skills of writer, directors, actors, composers, designers. But it also depends on the creative skills of the audience, those skills of the imagination that allow all of us to leap into other minds and other worlds, skills that are at once quite natural, straightforward, commonplace and quite quite amazing.

D.A.